Changeling Press. LLC
ChangelingPress.com

Bear/Ringo Duet
A Bones MC Romance
Marteeka Karland

Bear/Ringo Duet
A Bones MC Romance
Marteeka Karland

All rights reserved.
Copyright ©2026 Marteeka Karland

ISBN: 978-1-60521- 799-4

Publisher:
Changeling Press LLC
315 N. Centre St.
Martinsburg, WV 25404
ChangelingPress.com

Printed in the U.S.A.

Editor: Jean Cooper
Cover Artist: Marteeka Karland

The individual stories in this anthology have been previously released in E-Book format.

Table of Contents

Bear (Grim Road MC 5)
A Bones MC Romance
Marteeka Karland

Olivia: I've been sent to infiltrate Grim Road, specifically for any information to do with the man they call Bear. I didn't expect to jump into the man's arms on the first try. I also didn't expect to feel an illogical sense of belonging and safety when he whispered in my ear, "You're safe." My deception will probably get me killed. I'm not a damsel in distress, at least not how they think. But I think Bear knows I'm lying. He just doesn't seem to care.

Bear: Yeah, I know the girl's lyin'. I also happen to believe she has a good reason. If I can get her to trust me, then I can make her demons disappear. But trust is hard-earned. Even if I earn hers, can I trust her after she started out with lies? Do I really care if she's lying as long as she's mine? Trouble's following this girl. And it's headed straight to Grim Road.

Chapter One

Bear

I hated venturing out into the city. Always made me feel like there was a target on my fucking back. My true identity was buried so deep even facial recognition software couldn't find me, but since I'd been in my twenties, I'd spent my life running. The government saw to that.

What I thought was a service to help my country turned into a killing spree on the order of genocide. I'd disobeyed my orders but ended up on a Terminate with Extreme Prejudice list. Rocket, the closest person I had to a friend, had brought me to Riviera Beach, Florida, where I'd taken up with the motorcycle club, Grim Road. The club's history was long and distinguished in hiding men like me. I'd been here ever since.

It was nearly midnight on a Saturday. The streets weren't exactly teeming, but several bars were open, which was where most people were this time of night. Some headed home. Others milled about enjoying the evening air. It wasn't cool by any means, but the night brought in a breeze from the ocean that wasn't stifled by the heat of the sun during the day. This was my favorite part of the night.

"You lookin' for somethin' in particular, or just wishin' you could go back and change your life choices?" Ringo, our enforcer, sidled up next to me, handing me a beer.

"Thanks," I said as I popped the top and took a long swig. "Just thinkin'. Ain't much for bein' out of the compound."

"Oh, I know. Which is why I followed." The other man gave me a half smirk, half smile.

"Right. That, and Lemon probably told you to have my back."

He chuckled. "Little witch is certainly big on that kinda shit. But no. You'll be happy to know I did this all on my own."

I gave him a side eye. "Really. You tryin' to keep me honest? Afraid I'm out to betray the club?"

Instantly, Ringo's whole demeanor changed. "Hey, now. Jumping to conclusions there, Bear?" Ringo raised an eyebrow. "Of all the men in this club, you'd be the last one I'd accuse of betraying the club or anyone in it. Fully expected Rocket to make you his VP. I'd have supported that."

I snorted. "No way in fuckin' hell I want that job. Besides, Lemon is much better suited."

"Ain't sayin' she's not. Just sayin' I was surprised when Rocket didn't put your name in the hat for the job long before Lemon came on the scene."

The two of us headed down the sidewalk. Kind of felt like we were patrolling the area. There were several bars and clubs here, and some of them weren't altogether safe. A couple times a week, I'd taken to walking up and down the strip. I wouldn't say I was looking for trouble, but I wasn't opposed to stopping trouble if it found me. The self-imposed job got me out of the compound as well as extended some measure of protection to the community which pleased the VP to no end. I wouldn't exactly call the city *our* community, but I got the impression that's what Lemon wanted it to be. Crush and Byte worked continually to strengthen all our identity covers. Rocket wasn't opposed, so I took this as my due diligence. I was doing my part, however quietly, to set an example to the other members. It's how I did things.

"He offered." I shrugged. "Not my thing."

"Oh, really." The bastard smirked, and I wanted to beat the shit outta him, but restrained myself. Barely. "Was that before or after you corralled us all and put the idea of voting Lemon in as VP, or after?"

"Well, I wasn't gonna do it. Someone had to, and she was the best choice. You look me in the eye and tell me who else in Grim would be doing a better job than Lemon, and I'll volunteer that bastard."

Ringo chuckled. "Right. I'll get on that. But you have to promise you'll be the one to break the news to Lemon."

I snorted. "Not on your fuckin' life. Girl might be small and young, but she's vicious like no man I've ever met. You tell her your own Goddamn self."

We stared at each other a moment before Ringo's lips twitched. Once that happened, we both broke down into chuckles. Neither of us would be suggesting a replacement for Lemon.

The conversation eased something inside me. Like I *knew* Ringo had my back or something, where always before I'd kind of felt like I was on my own in the middle of a crowd. Yeah, I knew if I were really in trouble, outside of a mission, I could count on my brothers. Always had. But it was different now.

"Thanks, man. I think I needed that."

"For what? The reminder that a little five-foot-nothing girl is making a better vice president than you?"

I snorted. "No, dumbass. The laugh."

Ringo grinned. "Wait till I tell Lemon you were wanting to replace her."

"Whoa. Not cool, bro. Besides, it was you who brought it up. And I will totally throw you under the bus if you start that bullshit."

God, it felt good to banter with Ringo. I'd had

that kind of atmosphere a couple of times on jobs for the CIA, but it was never as relaxed as it was now.

I took a deep breath and rolled my head, easing some of the tension that always seemed to be there when I ventured too far from the compound. It wasn't that I was scared. It was more like I felt like someone was watching. Just waiting to make a move.

I could handle myself in an ambush. Fuck knew I'd been in that situation before and had come out on the other side. Worse for wear maybe, but the other guys fared far, far worse. Always.

Ringo snorted. "Glad to be of service, brother."

We continued down the street. The sound of people partying or generally having a good time filled the night. Each time we passed a bar, the scent of alcohol hit us. Occasionally someone would be smoking a joint or a cigarette and those scents would blend in as well. Passing a strip joint brought the cheap perfume into the mix.

I was about to suggest we go inside one of the strip clubs, just to pass the time with something different when I spotted a woman making her way down the sidewalk. Something about the way she moved was just that little bit off. She glanced behind her, then straight ahead. She hesitated, then continued moving.

"What's goin' on there?" I asked the question more to myself than to Ringo, but the other man zeroed in on the woman immediately.

"Not sure. Could be she's just lost."

"Right," I agreed, though I wasn't so sure. Something about her posture wasn't right. "Could be."

"Uh-huh."

We both continued forward but at a slower pace. Grim Road MC wasn't a secret club, per se. The club was known to the locals, just not where the clubhouse was or who any of us were beyond our road names. To everyone around us, we were simply another motorcycle club in the area around Palm Beach. As such, we wore our colors proudly. So, when the girl got closer to us, and we slowed down, we wanted her to know what we were.

I stopped while Ringo turned slowly around in a circle with his hands out, letting her see the emblem on the back of his vest proclaiming him a member of Grim Road.

She let loose a little sob and ran the rest of the way to us. To my complete and utter shock, instead of stopping when she reached us, the girl threw herself into my arms, wrapping her arms tightly around my neck.

And I'll be Goddamned if my whole body didn't come alive. Lust I'd never even dreamed about punched me in the dick before sucking me into its mouth and making me hard as a fucking pole. The scent of her was like something out of a dream. Fresh spring flowers and a dash of cinnamon. She was slender, but I could feel every single one of her slight curves against my big body. She was so small I could easily wrap my arms all the way around her with room to spare. Unfortunately, instead of moaning and finding my mouth with hers, she trembled in my arms. I didn't think it was from desire. Her mouth at my ear was a sinful promise. Until she spoke.

"Angela," she whimpered. "I need Angela."

"Hey, sweetheart," I said loudly. "Missed you, too." I chuckled, swinging her around happily. What I was really doing was putting my body between her and the two men I now saw following her.

I didn't acknowledge the men. Instead, I strode

down the sidewalk with her still in my arms. Ringo had my back. If he couldn't discourage the guys, I could get her far enough away she could get inside to the relative safety of a bar or club. Then, I'd help Ringo help these motherfuckers have themselves an accident.

When I rounded the corner with her, I set her on her feet, but kept hold of her hand. Everything inside me rebelled at the separation. I wanted to pull her solidly against me again but needed to make sure I had one hand free if Ringo needed me. Stepping from behind the wall, I eyed Ringo. He stood where I'd left him, but the men were already gone. Ringo took slow looks around the area as he backed toward me. I gave a low whistle, and Ringo turned and hurried in my direction.

"Get to the bikes." Ringo's order was delivered in a crisp voice. "They didn't keep following after you picked her up. You spoke and they backed off. Still don't want to take a chance."

"To Knox's place?" I knew we couldn't take her to the compound. Not without precautions. If the guys had truly backed off, she wasn't in immediate danger. If they hadn't, we'd reevaluate when we spotted them.

Ringo nodded. "I'll be on your six. Just gonna let Rocket know what's goin' on and that we'll call him when we know more."

I grunted, but tugged the woman with me and hurried to my bike. I snagged the helmet strapped to the back of my bike and shoved it on her head. Instead of waiting while she climbed on, I lifted her and set her on the back. "Feet on the pegs." I put her foot closest to me where I indicated and trusted her to do the same with the other one. Once I'd climbed on, I tugged her arms until they were around my waist. I wanted to tell myself it was for her safety. I mean, it was, but it was also because I wanted her mashed up against me. Needed it. *Craved* it. "Do not let go of me. Understand?"

"Yes." Her voice was soft and breathy, and she trembled. "Aren't you going to ask me any questions?"

"Yep," I said as I started up the bike and took off. I had plenty of fucking questions. Starting with how she knew the club's safe word for the women and what she expected to happen next. But not until me and Ringo were sure we were in a safe place with no immediate threats. Then we'd get to the bottom of this and find out what the woman expected to happen next. Because, if I had my way, once whatever threat she was facing was eliminated, I intended to get to know her a lot better.

* * *

Olivia

I clung to the truly massive biker in front of me like my life depended on it. And I mean fucking *huge*. Guy towered over my five-foot five frame like I was a child. He had at least a hundred and fifty pounds on me. The phrase I'd dropped on him had started a chain of events I knew I'd regret. Probably for the rest of my life, even knowing the rest of my life probably wasn't going to be very long. Lord knew this guy could break me in half with little more than a thought.

We rode through the back streets, taking several twists and turns. I thought there might have been a few double backs as well. In another situation, I'd have been having the time of my life. Not only was there a thrill riding on the bike, but the man…

He was big. Muscled. Tattooed. And, oh my God, he smelled *wonderful*. Cedar and sandalwood. And gasoline. I could feel the muscles of his abdomen rippling beneath my hands where I clung to him. In another world, without all the shit I was getting ready to bring down on his club, I could see myself trying to keep his attention focused on me. Being wrapped up tight in his arms had been the safest I'd felt in a very long time. It only lasted a few seconds, but the effect was profound. I'd do anything this man wanted. Follow wherever he wanted me to go. But that could never happen. Even if I knew he wouldn't take me over until I was a shell of myself, what I was about to do to his club would forever negate anything there might have been between us.

As if a man like this would ever want a woman like me. No. He'd want someone strong. Someone who fought for what was right, no matter the consequences to herself, instead of a little girl clinging to something toxic and dangerous just because it was familiar. Guess which one I was. Spoiler alert: it's not the former.

It wasn't until the other biker pulled up beside us and gave some kind of hand signal that we headed in a direction with purpose. The streetlights gave way to a darker, narrower road, and we seemed to disappear in the night.

A few minutes later, we pulled into the driveway of a ranch-style house with a porch running the length of the front. I didn't get a great look at it because it was too dark, but the windows were lit up from the inside as if someone was already there. The big biker drove straight into the open garage. The second both bikes were inside, the door closed, and they shut down their rides.

"Rocket, Lemon and Dom are already here," the other one said. "Inside."

Neither man spoke to me, but the one I'd thrown myself at helped me off the bike before taking my helmet. Then he took my hand and led me inside the house.

The second we entered the living room, Lemon moved in my direction. I'd never met her but there was no denying who she was. She was the harder version of her sister, Apple. Lemon narrowed her gaze at me. "I know you. You're Apple's friend. Liv? The one she told me she was worried about." She looked me up and down, taking in my appearance. "What happened?" I wasn't sure if she was talking to me or not, but was saved from asking with the big one, the one I'd rode here with, answered her question.

"She was being followed by two guys in suits. I first thought feds. They had that cheap, tired-looking suit thing goin' on, but coulda been the standard creepers." He shrugged. "Ringo showed his colors, and she ran straight to us."

"I got Crush lookin' at the camera feeds," the other one, Ringo, added. "He'll nail 'em down."

"Good." The man with Lemon nodded. "Now." He turned his gaze to me. "Do you know who we are?"

I nodded my head slightly. "A motorcycle club. Apple said it's called Grim Road. But other than Lemon, I don't know who anyone else is. Or anything." I spoke softly even as I trembled. I was so fucked. Even though this situation wasn't of my own making, I knew when it all came to a head, these people would probably kill me. OK, no probably about it. Hadn't Mr. Black told me these people were killers? They'd even killed innocent women and children! He'd said that one of them had even gone so far as to kill entire villages in third world countries where they'd been deployed. Just for amusement. Yeah. I was as good as dead. It was just a matter of time. I tried to think about those massacres when I steeled myself to do this, but I wasn't sure it helped. It probably made me as guilty as they were. So yeah. When they killed me, it would be no less than I deserved.

Lemon tilted her head. "Apple didn't tell you anything?"

"Only that if I ever got in a really tight spot, and I saw someone in a Grim Road vest, I could tell them I needed Angela and they'd know I was in danger."

"Good. OK. So, this is Rocket." She hiked a thumb toward the man beside her. "He's mine, so no touching." She waved to the man next to Rocket. "This is Dom. He's our sergeant at arms. The other two? The big one's Bear, the little one's Ringo. Ringo is our enforcer, Bear's... Bear."

"Little one, Lemon?" Ringo gave her a side eye and an exasperated huff. "Really?"

She shrugged. "Comparatively speaking. Now, shut up. I'm talking." Had my situation been less dire, I'd have been amused. Not now, though. Because when the shit hit the fan, this woman would likely be the one taking me apart. "What happened?"

I shivered, wrapping my arms around myself. "They followed me out of the bar."

Lemon tilted her head. "You with anyone?"

"No. I work there. I was on my way home and was afraid they'd follow me and know where I live."

"If they let you get home," Bear muttered, but he gave me a measured look. Like he wasn't really buying my story. "They speak to you? Threaten you?"

"Just trying to get me to stop so they could talk to me." I kept my gaze down, my arms wrapped around myself, trying to stop the trembling. "I'm sorry. I didn't mean to cause trouble. Or, you know, use a phrase I shouldn't have. Obviously, 'Angela' was intended to set in motion things for an extreme situation, and I wasn't in that much danger." Right. If only.

"Sounds like you were in plenty of danger," Lemon said. "You did exactly the right thing. The guys assessed the situation and got you out of there. End of story."

A phone beeped and Rocket pulled out his phone and glanced at the screen. "Crush says the guys following you are CIA. Not even trying to conceal their identity." He frowned, then looked up at me. "You got any idea why they wanted you?"

It surprised me they were so cavalier about being recognized. I really thought they'd try to hide themselves given how they said this group would go to any lengths to avoid the authorities. "Maybe my dad?" It was as close to the truth as I could get without blowing things. Besides I was a shit liar.

"What about your dad? Why would the CIA be looking into your dad?" Rocket was all business. Lemon too. Both of them were entirely focused on me and it fucking terrified me. If Lemon was anywhere near as observant and intuitive as her sister, this was over before it began. "He into something to be on their radar?"

"I don't know. He's been in some trouble with taxes or something," I said softly, shrugging.

"Honey, CIA don't do tax shit," Bear rumbled. He was so close beside me I swore I could feel the heat coming off his body.

I started, stepping sideways to get away from him. I didn't really want the distance, but knew I had to keep it. I wasn't good at this kind of thing and my wits being muddled because of my attraction to him would get me killed.

Bear didn't allow the retreat. Instead, he took one

slow, deliberate step closer, erasing the distance I'd put between us. I looked up into his face. His eyes seemed to bore a hole inside me with the intensity of his stare. This was someone I needed to be careful around. With my inability to lie worth a Goddamn and the way it felt like he could see into my soul, I'd be fucked before this even started.

"Back off, Bear." Rocket eased closer to the big man and put a hand on his shoulder. "She's frightened enough."

"She knows I ain't gonna hurt her." He didn't take his eyes from me. "You need to tell us everything. Finding out now is one thing. We're ready for it. But we find out you're bringin' a threat to us and not givin' us time to prepare? Well. That's totally different."

There was something in his eyes. Something that told me he was deadly serious. I could also see he was willing me to tell him the truth. Like it meant something to him if I told the truth or not beyond just keeping his club safe. No. This man *wanted* me to trust him. Which was something I could never do. Wasn't it?

For a moment, it was just the two of us. He looked into my face, placing a gentle hand on my shoulder to squeeze in encouragement. I wanted to believe him. To trust that he'd understand and not condemn me, and that he'd help me out of a really bad situation. I opened my mouth to tell him everything...

"I told you. I-I was scared of those g-guys following me h-home." I stumbled over my words. There was a doubt. One little doubt overriding my trust. What if...

I'd been told these guys wouldn't hesitate to kill me if they thought I was betraying them. While I had no doubt Apple believed they'd help me, I was scared to take that leap of faith. Not when there was more than my own life to think about.

The second I uttered the words, Bear's expression hardened and he stepped back. He didn't say anything else, but I could tell he was seeing through me. The thought terrified me. I took a shuddering breath, and hoped like hell it wasn't my last.

Chapter Two

Bear

She was lying. I'd bet my life on it. The question was, *why* was she lying? The terrified, vulnerable look in her eyes told me there was more to it than simply lying about what had happened tonight. Trouble was following this girl, and it was headed straight to Grim Road. I knew this like I knew none of it mattered. Not to me. This woman -- Olivia -- she was going to be mine.

Lemon sighed. "Right. OK. I guess we stay here." Yeah. Our VP knew she was lying, too.

Olivia backed up, moving away from all of us. "What does that mean?"

"Relax, buttercup," Lemon said, an annoyed look on her face. "No one's gonna hurt you, but we can't take you to the compound, and we can't leave you to your own devices when you're clearly lying about something to do with the way Bear and Ringo found you. So? Here we are and here we'll stay until Crush and Byte get a beat on the guys following you." She raised her eyebrows, giving Olivia a hard look. "Unless you change your story and tell us the truth."

"I'm not lying." She shook her head, her eyes wide and terrified. "I was afraid they'd follow me home."

"Bullshit," Lemon spat. Now, the VP was all business, not in the mood to fuck around. Olivia flinched, but Lemon didn't budge. She crossed her arms over her chest and leveled her piercing gaze on Olivia. "But I get why you'd be opposed to telling us what's really going on. For now. But we still can't let you leave until we know the truth."

She looked around at all of us. A trapped little

kitten unsure what to do. She was trembling where she stood, but shook her head slightly. "I understand." Her words were soft and resigned. Like she fully expected us to do something unspeakable but had accepted her fate.

"Christ," Dom swore, scrubbing a hand over his face. "Can't help you if we don't know what you're facin', girl," he muttered. Liv lowered her gaze to the floor and said nothing. "All right, then." Dom pulled out his phone. "Piston and Venus are in town. They'd be the best choice to stay with her anyway."

"I'll call Apple, too," Lemon said. "They're friends --"

"No! I don't want Apple." Olivia's head snapped up, her eyes wide and pleading as her gaze found Lemon's. Then she shook her head several times before continuing more sedately. "I mean, I'm sure she's busy." She looked away. "Or something."

Lemon's eyes narrowed as she studied the other woman. Then she nodded slowly. "All right. Venus and Piston it is."

"And me." No way I was staying out of this one. No fucking way.

"Not sure that's a great idea, Bear." Dom studied me carefully and I knew the man saw way more than I was comfortable with.

"I'm claiming her," I said. Why I said it I had no idea. Didn't change the facts, but I wasn't ready for this yet. Not by a long shot. The last thing I wanted to do was claim her, then have her be some kind of spy or informant or something. And I admitted to myself, if those guys really were CIA as Crush said, then, yeah. There was every possibility she'd brought the very people most of us were running from. Maybe not to our front door, but certainly close.

"No," Dom snarled, poking a finger against my chest. "You're not. You're gonna go home and let Venus and Piston deal with her until morning. After that, once Crush has had a chance to look into her and the whole situation, I'll reevaluate."

"You don't have a say in who I claim, Dom. My woman. My choice."

"I do when the safety of the club is involved. See this?" He pointed to the patch on his chest with his club designation. "Sergeant at arms means the safety of the club is my responsibility. That makes this every bit as much my choice as it is yours."

I took a step forward, but Lemon got between us. "Dump some testosterone, you guys. Bear." She gave me a hard stare. "If you take her as your woman, you've got to accept the consequences if she's not on the up and up. You willin' to do that?" It was times like this I seriously questioned whether Lemon was really a teenager. Sure, she'd adopted some of Rocket's mannerisms when dealing with tough business in and out of the club, but she was her own person with her own sense of moral toughness. The look on her face said she'd cut me herself if this went to shit, and not regret a Goddamned thing.

"I will."

"No!" Olivia gasped. "No. I, uh, I can't be your woman. I've... uh... I've already got a, uh, boyfriend."

"If he's the one who made you walk home on your own, he's useless." Besides, I knew she was lying. *Again.* This pattern was going to make it harder and harder to trust her when we got to that point.

"I wasn't walking home," she said, looking anywhere but at me or any of us. "I was walking to my car."

"Right. Baby, the employee parking lots in that

area are on the back side of the building. Where do you live? And, before you try to lie, keep in mind that Crush is looking into everything. Not only that, but you can't lie for shit."

She winced but shook her head. "I was walking back to my car." Her voice was quiet. Hell, I don't think even *she* expected us to believe her, but she was sticking to her story.

"All right, then," Lemon said. "I'll have the boys bring some food by. We've kept the place aired out and clean in case anyone needs a place to crash in the city, so you should be good here. Rocket will make sure Piston and Venus are on the way, so you'll have backup, Bear. Also, Ringo, put a couple more guys farther out to keep an eye on the place from a distance."

Rocket chuckled despite the situation. "It's almost like she thinks she's president, huh?"

Ringo snorted. "Don't give her ideas, prez. She'll have you retired and be runnin' the whole operation if you do."

"I already run the operation. I just let Rocket think he's in charge."

"As much as I'd love to deny it, she's probably right. She definitely knows how to manage me."

Lemon grinned up at our president. "Just one of the many reasons you love me."

"Absolutely," he said before pulling her to him and kissing her soundly. Which wiped the smirk off Lemon's face and put a dreamy smile there. Which she didn't even try to hide.

"Good luck." Ringo clapped my shoulder as he headed out the door. "Got a feelin' you're gonna need it."

Didn't I just know it.

Olivia wandered around the living/kitchen/dining area of the house. It wasn't a large place, but there was plenty of room for the two of us. Tomorrow, if things proved difficult and Venus and Piston needed to stay here with me, there would still be plenty of room. But I wasn't ready to give up yet. While I knew she was lying and that there was very likely some shit headed our way, I thought I could get through to her.

There was definitely an attraction between the two of us. I could tell she felt that pull. I also thought it went against her nature to lie. Not only was she shit at it, I didn't believe she wanted to. There was just something in her expression, like she felt guilty. It was all part of being a shit liar. So the question became, what or who was she protecting? The boyfriend she said she had? If so, it just proved she didn't need him. A woman should never have to protect her man. He should protect her, even at the expense of his own life. If it wasn't the boyfriend, then who? And why?

"You gonna talk?" Even though I'd spoken softly, she started, rubbing her hands up and down her arms.

Olivia shook her head, her gaze squarely in the middle of my chest. "I already told --"

"Yeah, you already told me a bullshit story." I took a quick step toward her. Of course, she retreated a couple more steps. What surprised me was she only took a couple of steps back. I knew how intimidating I was. I'd perfected the look in the most dangerous of situations. I backed her up to the wall and caged her in. "Now, you're gonna tell me the fuckin' truth."

"I've got nothing more to say." Her voice was a whisper, but I could tell she wouldn't budge. I wouldn't intimidate her into giving me what she wanted. Not yet anyway.

I pushed off the wall and stalking through the house, checking the doors and windows as I went. "Don't bother trying to leave. The house has an alarm, and the guys are set up outside in case you do. You won't get far." I stomped inside my bedroom, leaving the door open.

This was going to be tricky. Everything depended on what Crush found in the next twenty-four hours. By claiming Olivia, I'd be able to force the issue of taking her to the Grim Road compound if things got too hot to stay where we were. If it really was the CIA chasing her, the last thing we wanted to do was lead them straight to our home. But if she was in imminent danger, my claim would extend the club's protection to her. If we did, and she was a willing participant, then I'd share her punishment. So, the benefits to Olivia were way more than they were for me. Until she was well and truly mine anyway.

She'd followed me down the hall and I stopped in the doorway to the room I'd claimed. "You can have the room across the hall." I pointed. "It's bigger and has an adjoining bathroom. The doors stay open."

She blinked. "I... what?"

"You heard me. No shut doors except the ones leading outside. That means the bathroom too."

"I'm not leaving the bathroom door open." The look on her face was so incredulous I almost laughed. Now wasn't the time, though. I needed to be a hard-ass. She needed to trust me, but she also needed to know I absolutely would call her on her bullshit.

"Any door I find closed gets broken down. If that means I remove every fuckin' door in the place, that's what I'll do." I gave her my best "don't fuck with me" look. When she winced and turned away, I almost felt bad. Almost. This was for her own good. "Now. If you want a shower and stuff before bed, get to it. You had supper?"

"I'm not hungry," she whispered. "Thank you. I'm sorry. For everything. I didn't mean to cause so much trouble." Did I imagine she winced again? Regret this time instead of fear? Guilt, beyond just the lying she'd already done? I'd always thought of myself as a good judge of character, but since the whole fucking mess with Hammer and Claw I always questioned myself. I did now too, but I knew it didn't matter. Not really. I wanted Olivia for my own. No matter the situation. So I had to really be careful, to unwind her lies to my satisfaction without breaking her. Which... yeah. This was going to be tricky.

"You ain't no trouble, honey. But you do need to trust me. Tell me what's goin' on. We can't protect you if we don't know what the fuck's happenin'."

Instead of answering, she turned and went into the room I'd indicated was hers. She put her hand on the door, then dropped it, looking over her shoulder. If she was looking for permission to shut it, she was dead wrong. I just gave her a look. She sighed and continued in.

"Fine. Venus will be here soon with some more stuff. For now, there should be a complete change of clothes in the duffel in the corner over there." I pointed next to the bathroom. "I'm serious when I say no closed doors. I will break a motherfucker down."

"I know," she said softly. Then she crossed to the duffel and entered the bathroom. She didn't shut the door.

I scrubbed a hand over my face as I stomped inside the room I'd claimed across the hall. There was a queen-size bed, dresser, nightstand, and little else. I could hear the shower running in the other room and knew she needed to scrub the day off her.

I sat on the bed, my mind seizing on Olivia, naked in the shower. Not a great idea. The very last thing I needed to do was get distracted by my dick. There was no denying she was a beautiful, desirable woman. But I didn't like secrets. Which was hypocritical because I'd kept my share over the years. Still had them. But I knew in my soul I'd never allow this woman to keep secrets from me. For the first time, I truly understood why Lemon insisted we stop with the secrets thing. We couldn't keep the club safe if we all had secrets that could come back to haunt us. And I couldn't keep my woman safe if I didn't know what was haunting her.

I sat on the bed, not daring to leave her alone. There was every possibility she was contacting someone, letting them know where she was and the situation. If that was true, Crush would know and we'd deal with it. That wasn't the reason, though. It took everything I had in me not to strip off and join her in that shower. Not for sex, though I really wanted that. Very fucking much. I wanted to dominate her. To have her riding the edge until she was so mad with lust she told me everything just to fall over the fucking edge.

Yeah. I was fucked sideways. To hell and back.

Chapter Three

Olivia

I was so fucked. Not only was I alone in a house with the scariest man I'd ever seen, but I was crazy attracted to him. And he would likely kill me when he figured out what I was doing, because that's what he did. He was a straight-up killer. I wouldn't blame him either. I was sacrificing these men and women to save myself.

OK, so that wasn't exactly true. I was sacrificing them to save my father, even though he didn't deserve saving. Especially not at the expense of these people. People who went out of their way to help a perfect stranger because she'd indicated she was in danger. Mr. Black had been right. He was the one who'd told me all I had to do was play the damsel in distress, and this bunch would bring out the big guns. Grim Road had certainly gone way the hell out of their way to help me. I tried to cling to what Black had told me about them. That they'd basically killed villages of people, multiple villages, in countries where no one cared, just because they could.

Water sluiced off my skin under the cascade in the shower. He was right that I wanted to freshen up, but it wasn't to wash off my day. It was to wash off his scent. The longer I smelled him, the more under his spell I fell. I wanted to trust him, to tell him anything he wanted to know, which wasn't like me. I'd learned early on to keep my head down and my mouth shut. All because of my father.

I shivered. They'd threatened my father, and my father had threatened me if I didn't do as they asked. While I might want to leave him, to tell this group of warriors everything and hope they'd save me, his threat that someone worse than the feds would turn their sights to me was what I was worried about most. I knew my father was into bad shit and I'd said nothing, helping him run the company because he knew my brain would serve his business better than my body would serve his associates. My mother hadn't been so lucky. If I betrayed Black and ended up here with the people I'd intended to spy on... was that the "something worse" my father had been alluding to? There was no doubt in my mind once they found the extent of what I was doing, leading Mr. Black and his associates straight to them, they'd make me suffer.

I took my time in the shower, not really washing so much as letting the water fall over me. I hadn't looked through the duffel yet. There wasn't any soap or shower gel in here anyway. Besides, I didn't really want to wash off Bear's scent. Not like I should want to, anyway. No. This was my one time to feel sorry for myself before I had to suck it up again. I could do this. This would not break me. The situation wouldn't anyway. But the resulting guilt and self-loathing might. These people didn't deserve my betrayal, and I had no idea how I was going to follow through. Maybe it was time to consider my options. Maybe I could find a way out before I did something unforgivable.

With a sigh, I turned off the water and snagged the towel I'd thrown over the top of the shower. With the door open, I wasn't getting out without covering up. Despite my attraction to him and how safe I'd felt in his arms before, the fact was I didn't know this man. I didn't think Apple would have told me to call a group of men who'd hurt me when I was already in trouble, but who really knew?

I stepped out of the shower and peeked around. Bear wasn't in sight, so I poked my head out the door of the bathroom to the main bedroom. Not there either. This might be my one chance to do what I was supposed to before they took my phone. And I knew they'd take it eventually. If they did, it would all be over. My life would change forever, but maybe Grim Road wouldn't be affected. That would take the pressure off me, take the decision out of my hands.

My clothes were still in the bathroom where I'd removed them. There was an app I was supposed to activate when I got to the clubhouse, but it looked like I wasn't gonna make it there. So I activated it now. It was supposed to give the men who had my father access to anything electronic that used Wi-Fi, Bluetooth, or cell service. I had no idea how it worked. They'd had to give me a special phone, but it had been my only instruction. They didn't care if I got out of the compound or not. Only that I gave them access to it and its location.

It wasn't long before the phone buzzed. I winced. I'd been instructed that I had to answer the phone when they called or they'd assume I'd been compromised and would come in guns blazing. In that scenario, they'd assured me no one would live.

"Hello?"

"You're not in the fuckin' compound? Why'd you turn it on?" I had no idea what the man's name was, only that he called himself Mr. Black. I was pretty sure his heart was black. I knew for sure he wasn't on my side even if he said he was some kind of federal officer. He didn't care if something happened to me. To him, I was as guilty as my father, no matter the circumstances, if he thought about me at all. More correctly, I was a pawn to be used and sacrificed in whatever game he and whomever he worked for were playing.

"They won't take me to the compound. This is the best I can do." I tried to keep my voice down. The last thing I needed was Bear to hear me talking to someone and come to investigate.

"You better fuckin' figure out a way to get there. When you do, restart your Goddamn phone and do it again."

"You know they're not going to let me keep my phone. That'll be the first thing they take if they decide to take me there."

"Then I suggest you figure out a way to keep it, or your father is a dead man. And I'll see your ass gets sent to Gitmo. You just think what these bastard bikers would do to you would be bad. Accidentally get lost on the male side of the *that* place and see what happens." The line went dead, the threat clear.

I shook as I hid the phone in the duffel they'd brought clean clothes to me in, keeping my dirties separate, so they wouldn't have a reason to dig through the bag. Bear had been right. There was a complete change of clothes, including panties still in the pack and toiletries that hadn't been opened.

I dressed in loose pants and a T-shirt. They were a little big, but comfortable. For tomorrow, there was another shirt and a pair of jeans, socks, and shoes.

Yeah. The people who'd put together this duffel for me on a moment's notice were the people I was supposed to betray. This is what my life had finally come to. Could I actually do this? Would the price be worth the actual cost? Because I was beginning to truly believe my life wasn't worth betraying these people.

I leaned forward, placing my hands on the vanity. Taking a deep breath, I tried to lift my head, to look myself in the mirror but couldn't. If I did this, if I followed the instructions I was given to save my father and myself, I had no doubt I'd be condemning good people. Maybe not to death, but the way Mr. Black had spoken about them, it wouldn't surprise me.

"Olivia?" Bear leaned against the door frame leading to the bathroom. I turned, brushing my fingers under my eyes to catch the tears before he saw me. "What the fuck's goin' on, honey?" This time, his voice was gentle. Not like before when I lied to him.

"I'm just shook up's all. I'm fine." I smiled but couldn't meet his gaze. Tears threatened even more but I managed to keep them under control. "I'm really sorry to put you all through this."

He straightened and stalked toward me. Where he'd pounced on me before, now he was patient, careful. He wore a black, short-sleeved T-shirt that seemed to mold every muscle in his chest and abdomen. Veins snaked up his forearms while the one in his bicep disappeared into the stretched cotton of his shirt. Tattoos covered one arm almost entirely while the other one had what looked like a snake wrapped from his wrist to his elbow. Made me wonder what the rest of him looked like when my thoughts had no business going there.

"That's the first truth you've told me so far. That you're sorry to put us through this." He took another step toward me. Now, he was in my personal space. "My question is, what exactly are you putting us through?"

I backed up a step and he followed. When my back hit the vanity, Bear grabbed my waist and lifted so that I sat on the counter next to the sink. Answering him was difficult, but I knew he expected an answer; though if he was as good at reading me as he seemed to be, it wouldn't be the answer he wanted.

"Dropping everything to come out here. Bringing

me clothes. That kinda trouble." It wasn't a lie, exactly. I did regret interrupting their lives, but it wasn't the whole truth.

He scowled. "There you go again." He stepped close, wedging his hips between my legs. He still had his hands on my waist, refusing to give me any space. "But don't worry. We'll get there."

I shook my head. "There's nothing more to tell."

This time he chuckled, his arms sliding around me as he pulled me more firmly against him. My whole body threatened to go up in flames. God, in another life... Yeah. If I'd met Bear even two months ago, when I'd first met Apple, I might have given him whatever he wanted if I could be in this position, with him touching me and his body so very close.

"I can tell when you lie. Like I said. You ain't worth a shit at it." He spoke softly, almost gently.

The next thing I knew, Bear's lips were pressed gently to mine. Teasing. Coaxing. Tempting. I couldn't prevent the whimper that escaped. I clutched his shirt, fisting the material tightly to ground myself. This man could very easily take me over and get around my defenses. I had to be very careful. But how the hell could I be careful when I'd never experienced anything like this in my life?

"You feel it too," he whispered against my lips. "Don't you." It wasn't really a question. Bear knew how he affected me. Had likely planned this exact situation to get me to lower my inhibitions and surrender to him. Which I could never do. If I did, I'd lose the only family I had left, and probably my life as well.

Even knowing what was at stake, I couldn't pull away from that kiss. His hand slid through my hair, bunching the strands in his fist and angling my head where he wanted me. God help me, I didn't even try to fight him.

He nipped my bottom lip, and I opened on a gasp, edging my legs wider around his hips. Bear growled his approval and deepened the kiss, thrusting his tongue inside my mouth with a wicked flick. I welcomed him, soaked up the attention, even knowing this was all designed to get my compliance. He wanted my secrets and was willing to do anything at his disposal to get what he wanted. Including using my body against me.

It should have been easy to push away from him knowing he was just one more person trying to manipulate me into doing something I didn't want to do. But, giving up the pleasure he effortlessly created inside me, and the closeness I felt from that intimate kiss, was the hardest thing I'd done in my life to this point.

I ducked my head, breaking the kiss and immediately felt the loss. Instead of letting me go, however, Bear pressed his forehead to mine. It was then I realized he was breathing just as hard as I was.

"Tell me you don't feel it too," he dared. "Because I don't think you can lie about this. Not even to yourself."

"I may be attracted to you, but that doesn't mean I trust you."

His low chuckle vibrated through me, sending a shudder racing down my spine.

"Ain't askin' for your trust, sweetheart. You're gonna give it to me. Willingly."

"You're delusional," I scoffed, but I couldn't hide the way my voice trembled or the way my nipples peaked against my T-shirt.

Bear looked amused. "Probably. But I stand by

my opinion. I'll get you there."

With a slow, deliberate movement, Bear stepped back away from me. That dark stare of his was molten, burning me from the inside out. Then he turned and strode out of the room. His footsteps weren't heavy, but I heard him move out of my bedroom and across the hall to his own. My heart pounded and my whole body tingled.

Yeah. I'd been right. I was so fucked.

Chapter Four

Bear

That kiss was a mistake. Probably the biggest mistake I'd made in my life. That kiss sealed my fate for good or ill. Olivia was lying her ass off. She was bringing something bad to the club and refused to say what. Which meant she'd have to be dealt with. Which meant... shit just got real.

I took several deep breaths as I sat on the bed. I needed to get a fucking grip. Now. Pulling out my phone, I shot off a text to Rocket. He was my oldest friend, the reason I was here in the first Goddamned place instead of in an unmarked grave or some shit in a little country on the other side of the world.

Me: *Gonna need this whole thing expedited.*

Rocket: *Figured. Calling you now.*

Seconds later my phone rang.

"Byte says one of the guys following her was your handler in Libya." There was a pause while Rocket let that sink in. All I could do was gasp in a breath. "Yeah. Thought you might want to know that. What do you want to do?"

"You're asking me?" I was incredulous that he'd even ask me that question. "You know what we have to do," I snapped. "That's a fuck of a lot bigger than simply leadin' the feds to our door. We've killed people for less."

"So, that's what you want to do?"

"Why are you making it sound like this is my decision, Rocket? You're the fuckin' president. Hell, your woman'll make it if you can't."

There was a silence while I took a moment to process that I'd just called out the one man I trusted with my life, same as accusing him of not being able to make hard decisions.

"Yeah," Rocket drawled, but his tone of voice said he was barely restraining himself. If I was standing in front of him right then, I was sure he'd punch me. "I'm gonna forget you said that. I can absolutely make the hard decisions. The only reason I'm not now is because you claimed her, you bastard. And I absolutely will not pass a snap judgment on one of our old ladies. I'm extending the same courtesy to Olivia because of you."

"Why? What do you expect to gain? She's guilty. Not like we didn't expect it."

"And you took responsibility, Bear. Means the kill's yours."

"Name the time and place, Rocket." The words burned in my throat. This should be an easy task. After all, I'd known this woman a couple of hours at best. I claimed her because I'd never had such a strong reaction to a woman. Not after knowing her for weeks or months. Certainly not on first sight. Even though I tried to act like I could kill Olivia if Rocket said it had to be done, I wasn't so sure I could.

"Uh-huh." Yeah. Rocket was calling bullshit. "Here's what's gonna happen. Strip search her. Venus and Piston should be there shortly. Tell Venus. Olivia takes nothing with her but the clothes we give her. Bring her to the compound and we'll lock her down until the boys work this out."

I grunted, but didn't acknowledge Rocket in any other way, disconnecting the call. I'd set myself up for this. All the way around. Any discomfort I felt was my own fault for getting carried away. Hell, if Leon Black was her handler, he'd likely handpicked Olivia for me. The man knew me almost as well as Rocket did. Rather, he used to know me that well. I'd changed.

Being set up to be killed on the other side of the world would do that to a person.

I sat there, thinking, trying to process what I was feeling. I never had such a strong reaction to a woman -- or any person for any reason -- in my life. I'd known her a couple hours. I knew nothing about her, except she was likely a mole. Even worse, Leon Black, the fucking bastard, was fucking with my head. Again. Only this time, he'd dangled something in front of me I had no hope of resisting. I didn't know if he'd done it intentionally or not, but I was sure as hell going to find out. First things first, though. Once Piston got here with Venus, we'd pack out the trash and hit the trail. Back to Grim Road.

When my anger faded to become a little more manageable, I stood and went through the house to the living room to wait for Piston. No need to be angry at Olivia. I'd known she was involved in something she didn't want us to know about. Even told her I knew she was lying. I put myself in this situation. Which meant I had to tell that asshole, Ringo, he was right.

Stupid.

Stupid, stupid, *stupid*!

I wanted to get on my bike and just... *ride*! Mainly because the craziest thing about this whole situation was that I still wanted to protect Olivia. I still wanted her to be mine, and I meant to get to the bottom of this. Before the end -- whatever the end might be -- I would know exactly what was going on with Leon Black and what part Olivia was playing. And why.

I expected that monstrosity of a pink Harley Venus rode, but she and Piston pulled up in a black Bronco.

They entered the house, and Piston shook my

hand in a firm grip. "Heard you needed a babysitter."

"Somethin' like that." I glanced at Venus. "You talked to Rocket or Lemon?"

"*Da*. Lemon filled me in. We brought fresh clothing even though she had some in bag Lemon brought. I'm to search her. Make sure she has only clothes I give her."

"Crush came with us." Piston hiked a thumb over his shoulder in the general direction of the Bronco. "Brought some fancy-schmancy electronic shit. Said he'll be scannin' her person as well as anything she's had contact with before we leave."

I glanced down the hall to find Olivia standing in the hallway in the cotton pants and tee Lemon had brought. When she backed up a step, like she was going back into her room, Venus stopped her.

"Stop," she barked. "From this moment on, you do not leave my sight." She walked down the hall, not intimidating in the least in her pink leather. If you didn't take into account she was over five-nine and solidly built. A delicate flower Venus was not. Oh. And she had razor-sharp pink nails. And pink hair.

And pink eyes.

Olivia's gaze darted to me. Whatever she saw there must have clued her in to the fact I wasn't pleased. She didn't say anything, though, and she followed Venus's instructions. Ducking her head, she entered the bedroom with Venus right behind her.

I wanted to protest, to go to Olivia and do this myself but I knew that one, I didn't trust myself not to take out my anger on her and be rougher with her than I should. And two, Olivia would never look at me the same way again if I forced her to strip in front of me. Not in this situation.

Piston's amused snort brought my attention

away from Olivia. "What's so fuckin' funny?"

"You. How long you known that girl?"

"I don't."

"Yeah? Why'd you claim her?"

I shrugged. "Seemed like a good idea at the time."

Piston crossed his arms over his chest. The man might be in his late fifties, but he was still solidly built and way more intuitive than I liked. "Yeah? How's it feel now?"

"Like fuckin' shit." I scrubbed a hand over my face. "Fuck."

"Yeah. I know the feelin'."

I barked out a short laugh. "You do, huh? How do you figure?"

Piston nodded to the door Venus and Olivia had disappeared behind. "You think I got it made with that one? She's mine, but she's fightin'. And let me tell you, those nails of hers are sharper than they look."

"Really? Because they look fuckin' sharp to me."

"Exactly." Piston grinned. "Always did like to live dangerously."

"You're nuts, old man."

"Yeah? I'm not the one who claimed a woman the first time I laid eyes on her."

"Exactly how long had you known Venus when you claimed her?"

"That's different. I might not have known her, but I knew what she was. What she stood for." Again, he nodded to the hallway and the bedroom. "You don't know nothin' about that one."

"I know she's working for my CIA handler. The man who sent me on a suicide mission because I refused to follow bullshit orders."

Piston whistled low. "Not a great start, brother."

"Yeah. Tell me something I don't know."

"All right. How about this." The older man leaned one hip against the door facing. "Apple says she's sure someone is hurting Olivia. Maybe not physically, but mentally. Emotionally. Terrorizing that young woman."

I shook my head. "Ain't goin' there, Piston. Whatever reason she has, she had a chance to come clean and she didn't take it."

He shrugged. "All I'm sayin' is find all the facts. Look as deep as you can. Lemon and Apple are... special. Everyone knows it. Lemon's found her way and is on the path that suits her. Apple hasn't yet, but she needs to help people. Ever since the thing with Scarlet, Apple's changed. Whatever happened at Iron Tzars with that man of hers made it worse. What she saw in Olivia was bad enough she gave her the club safe word. She was also demanding to come here to be with Olivia."

"What?" I snapped the question, narrowing my eyes. "She's not, right? Because that would be the one person Olivia could hide behind and keep us away from her. If she puts Apple between herself and us, she's got us by the balls."

"Idiot," Piston muttered. "You really need to learn to watch a woman for a while before you go all caveman Neanderthal and put your claim on her. You don't know a Goddamned thing about this woman. Do you?"

"What the fuck is it with everyone telling me what woman I can or can't claim?"

"Never said you couldn't claim her. Just that you're a dumbass for taking a look at a pretty face and deciding to spend your life with the woman."

"Christ, Piston. I feel something for her or I

wouldn't have done it. There's a... I don't know. A pull to her."

"I see." He sighed. "Well, good luck, boy. You're in for a bumpy ride."

* * *

Olivia

"I'd apologize in advance, but I think you knew this or something like it was coming." The woman who'd escorted me into the bedroom and shut the door was all business. Judging by her expression, there would be absolutely no give to her.

"Strip down to underwear." She had a moderately thick Russian accent in a pleasing contralto. Judging by all the pink, I was pretty sure this was Venus. Apple had told me about her a couple of times, always with an admiring grin. Like, if she thought she could pull it off, she'd emulate the woman's look but thought it might be a bit much. Venus stood back at a reasonable distance, not getting up in my space or making me feel threatened. Which told me I had absolutely no chance of getting away from her even if I tried.

"Any clothes I have on were given to me by your club. Why do I have to strip now?"

She tossed another complete change of clothing onto the bed and set a pair of canvas shoes on the floor. Everything looked to be brand-new, socks and underwear still in the packs. "Because, we don't take chances with our home." She leveled a look on me. "*Any* chances."

With a sigh, I did as she instructed. Venus was respectful but firm, averting her eyes for the most part and only watching me when it was strictly necessary. Each article of clothing I discarded, Venus checked.

And I mean, she *checked*. Pockets, of course, were turned inside out. The woman went around the hemmed seam, feeling for anything between the fabric folds.

Once that was done, she nodded at me. "Now underwear. Unfasten your bra and I'll hand you new one so you're not exposed more than necessary."

I cringed. "Do you really have to be that thorough?" I thought I might be in trouble here, but it wasn't any more than I expected. The only thing I had was the phone. I was supposed to keep a small journal for observations, but I didn't have anything for it yet. And I wasn't really sure I could now. How was I supposed to rat on these people when they were being so kind? I mean, the strip search was a little much, but if they were really serious about keeping their location secret, then I guess I understood it. Besides, I'd known this was coming.

Again, each time I gave her an article of clothing, Venus searched it thoroughly. She didn't give me privacy to change, but she didn't make it weird either. Once I had the new underwear on, she handed me a pair of cotton Capri pants and a black tank top which I put on quickly.

The next thing she did was pick up the duffel I'd been given with the other change of clothes. And my phone.

She unzipped the duffel and dumped the contents out onto the bed. It was like the phone was just waiting to be found because it bounced off the bed and onto the floor with a soft *thud*. Venus didn't look at me or in any way indicate she was displeased, but she stuffed the phone into her back pocket before going over the rest of the clothing in the duffel.

"You know, your people gave me those clothes.

They've only been here a couple of hours and not out of the house since they've been in my possession."

"*Da.* But they don't take chances with their home. Especially when woman they bring back was running from CIA agent." She gave me what looked like a genuine smile, but I couldn't be sure. Like this wasn't even an inconvenience. Just an everyday occurrence.

"How long have you been with Grim Road?"

She shrugged. "I'm not really with them. Piston has idea I'm his woman, but I haven't made up my mind."

"You don't like him?"

"I like him plenty. It's whole relationship thing. Though since my sister, Millie, let herself get caught up with man, I see it isn't always a situation where woman doesn't have control. Millie and Shadow have very balanced relationship." Her smile broadened as she spoke about the couple. "He is good man. Lets Millie be herself without trying to stifle her."

"Is Piston that way with you?"

She shrugged. "Mostly. Sometimes he forgets I've killed more people than he has and tries to shelter me." Venus shook her head, amusement dancing in those creepy pink eyes of hers. I also thought the casual statement she'd just dropped had been anything but casual. She'd intended it as a warning. "Those times are strangely amusing to me." She folded each article of clothing as she talked, placing them neatly back inside the bag. "Shall we go?"

I took a breath and nodded.

Venus extended her arm for me to go ahead of her.

Chapter Five

Bear

Once Venus opened the door for Olivia to enter the main room of the house, my gaze zeroed in on her. Venus gave a curt nod in my direction. I narrowed my eyes at her before glancing back to Olivia.

"You let her keep phone?" Venus pulled the device from her back pocket and tossed it to me.

"Didn't search her," I said as I easily snagged the phone out of the air. "Didn't want her to feel threatened, and it didn't really matter. This place isn't secret and if we stayed here very long, I'm sure they'd find us with or without her help."

"Fine. We ready to move?"

"*Da.*" Venus turned to Olivia. "You will ride with me and Piston. Apple is anxious to see you." Venus actually gave Olivia a friendly, if small, smile.

Olivia opened her mouth to say something but shut it before she did and nodded crisply. "Very well." Then she preceded Venus outside.

I followed, meeting Crush behind the Bronco Piston and Venus had brought. Crush's bike was a classic Harley Softail. The younger man had bought it off Red at Salvation's Bane, and I was pretty sure he wanted to make love to that bike.

Crush stepped forward and shook my hand. "I've got Byte working on this from the command center." That's how we referred to his and Byte's office. We were joking. Crush wasn't. "I'll take her phone off-site and take it apart. Inside and out. Any data on that phone I'll extract."

"Good. And Crush? Let me know the second you find something."

Crush gave me a steady look. "You know I gotta

tell Rocket or Lemon first, but you'll be right behind them." This is what I liked about Crush. He and Byte were both like this. He absolutely would not lie. No matter what. At least, if he ever had, I'd never caught him. Both men always let you know where you stood with them and where they stood with you. There was no sugar coating, no false promises.

"Just do what you can." There was no use pushing Crush. He'd do what he felt was right. For him to call me ahead of Rocket would be against his personal code.

"I will. I'll also have Knox send someone for your bike."

"Thanks, man. Tell him not to send Falcon. Bastard's had his eyes on my bike since Lemon painted his."

"Probably wondering if he could get away with painting yours pink so he could paint his black again." One corner of his lips curled upward.

I snorted. "Yeah. Likely."

Crush pocketed the phone, then started his bike and took off.

Venus held open the door to the back seat of the Bronco while Piston stood with his arms on the open door and top of the vehicle, his foot propped on the running board on the driver's side. He kept watch, scanning the surroundings intently, looking for a threat.

I climbed in the back seat on the driver's side so that Olivia was sandwiched between me and Venus. She glanced at me nervously before swallowing and fumbling with the middle seat belt. I could feel her trembling where my shoulder and thigh pressed against her.

"One last time, Liv," I growled next to her ear.

"What's goin' on?"

She didn't respond, just clenched her teeth and pursed her lips. One tear escaped and trickled down her cheek, but she didn't acknowledge it.

I sighed and straightened in my seat. "You will, Liv. Eventually, you will." I didn't raise my voice or even look at her, but I could feel her stiffen. I wanted her scared, but it nearly gutted me to do it deliberately. I could very well be pushing her away from me when I wanted to do anything but. It was as much for her safety as the club's.

If I was honest, it might be more for her than Grim. And I didn't mean that she'd be in danger from Grim. It was Leon Black. The bastard would stop at nothing to find me. I was the one blemish on an otherwise perfectly stellar career for him. He'd managed to deflect the blame to someone else, but the stain still followed him behind closed doors since it'd happened.

So, yeah. I was very concerned for Olivia's safety. Well, that was about to be fixed. I was taking her to Grim Road to stay with me. I'd prove she could trust me and I'd work on trusting her.

Piston pulled a blindfold and a hood from the console and handed them to me. I carefully placed the blindfold over Liv's eyes and the hood over her head to prevent her from seeing where we were going. The back windows were darkly tinted, so no one could catch a good glimpse of us in the back seat. Piston took back streets and made several direction changes as he took us to the club house.

Piston's phone rang. Venus picked it up and answered.

"*Da.*" There was a silence before Venus disconnected the phone. "Byte says all clear. We go back to clubhouse."

We were always careful about returning home, but Piston and Byte were assuming we were actively being followed. He even left the road at one point and went through the wetlands and back trails before Byte gave him the all clear. When we got to the clubhouse, it was by way of the back of the property.

* * *

Olivia

The second I was able to ditch the hood and blindfold and climb out of the vehicle, I spotted Apple. She ran full force, shoving her way through the big men scattered around us, and threw herself at me.

"Liv! I was so worried! Thank God you ran into Bear and Ringo!" Apple hugged me fiercely, not letting me go even when someone tried to pull her off me.

"I'm OK, Apple." I patted her back a couple of times before gently pushing her away. When I did, one of the men kept her moving away from me. "It's OK." I sounded like I was consoling someone while on the way to the execution chamber. Because I knew absolutely it was not OK.

"Come on," Bear said, taking my hand. "You can spend time with her once this is cleared up."

I could see Apple arguing with Leather. He was steadily leading her back to the club house, not forcing her or being overly aggressive, simply moving her away calmly as he spoke to her. I didn't know Apple that well, but she'd seen the end of an argument I'd had with my father and Mr. Black. Apple had marched toward us and grabbed my hand, telling the pair to fuck off while she took me to a local diner and offered me a place to stay. That was the first time we met.

The next time I'd met Apple, it had been with a

black eye and a busted lip. While the first encounter had been an accident, the second one hadn't. And I'd suffered through it in silence.

Bear took me to a small house a short distance away from the clubhouse. We walked, my hand firmly in his. We could almost have been a couple out for a stroll under the moonlight. Except for the elephant hanging over us.

He ushered me inside. I wouldn't say it was dirty or anything, but it was definitely a man cave. It was messy with beer cans and pizza boxes on more than a few surfaces. But the couch and chairs were free of clutter. There were no dishes in the sink or dirty clothes laying around on the hardwood flooring, and the place smelled clean.

"Fuckin' prospects," Bear muttered. He pulled out his phone, selected a contact and put the phone to his ear. Whoever he called answered almost immediately. "You tell that little punk, Redwood, to get his fuckin' punk-ass friends over here and clean up my place. If it ain't exactly how I left it in thirty minutes, Imma kill every single one of them motherfuckers. And if there is even one thing out of place in my bedroom, it won't matter if they get my place clean." He stabbed at the phone's screen, disconnecting the call. "Motherfuckers," Bear muttered under his breath.

He scrubbed a hand over his face, then turned his attention to me. "Same rules apply here. No shut doors except those leading outside. House has an alarm that goes straight to Crush and Byte, so we'll have you back before you reach the perimeter."

"I understand." I refused to meet his gaze. Bear already knew my tells. He knew when I was lying.

There was silence. I wrapped my arms around

my body as I stood there, unsure what to do next. Bear shuffled around the room, picking up beer cans and bottles despite sending for the people who'd apparently made the mess. He didn't say anything until there was a knock at the door.

"Thank Christ," he muttered, then stomped to the door and yanked it open. Three younger men stood outside. All of them looked ready to piss themselves.

"Sorry, Bear," one of them said. "We were comin' back to clean up but thought we had more time. You said you'd be back in the morning."

"So the first lesson you better have learned is not to put shit off. When you have a job to do, you fuckin' do it."

"And we never went nowhere except in here and the bathroom," one of the others said as he picked up a nearby box and started moving through the room. "And no whores, Bear. We was just watchin' the game. I swear." The guy didn't much more than look at Bear. He was picking up everything out of place and tossing it into a big-ass contractor trash bag.

"How could you guys have eaten so much pizza during the fuckin' game anyway?"

The third guy had a cocky smirk as he leaned against the door. "We're growin' boys, Bear. Got all kinds of…" He paused and turned his gaze to me, his smile widening to a lascivious grin. "Voracious appetites."

Bear lunged for the younger, smaller man and grabbed him by the throat in what looked like a crushing grip. The guy went for something at his hip. Bear was all up in his face, so I was certain there was no way he knew what was happening.

"Bear! Knife!" The words popped out of my mouth before I could stop them. I even lunged to grab the guy's hand as he came out with the knife.

There was a scuffle as one of the men was pulling at the guy with the knife, the other trying to pry Bear's hand loose.

"Drop it, Redwood!"

"He's gonna strangle him to death, French!" This was the guy trying to pull Bear off the guy they called Redwood.

"If he does, Wood deserved it." French grunted as he managed to get the knife away from Redwood. In the process, my arm got in the way and the knife laid a fiery gash along the underside of my forearm.

I gave one sharp cry, backing away. Then I clamped my mouth shut and slapped a hand over the wound. Bear immediately turned to me, dropping his gaze to where blood seeped between my fingers and dripped to the floor.

"Fuckin' Christ." He let go of Redwood, not bothering to look at the man. "What the fuck did you mean to do, girl? Fight off a man twice your size -- with a knife -- using only your bare hands?" He snagged my arm, putting his own huge hand over the wound as he moved us to the sink. "Banjo, get that bastard out of my sight. Tell Rocket or Lemon what happened. Let them deal with the little prick." He refused to turn toward the men, instead pulling out a dish towel from a drawer and wrapping it around the cut to stop the bleeding.

"Consider it done, Bear," Banjo pushed Redwood toward the door.

"You tell 'em everything. Not just that I busted his ass. You tell 'em why. You tell every fuckin' horny-ass prospect in this fuckin' compound. 'Cause this ain't fuckin' over." Bear did turn to look at the other men then. "Best make your peace with whatever God you believe in, you son of a bitch."

"I swear I didn't know she was yours, Bear," Redwood pleaded, his eyes wide. "I'd never have said that if I'd known she was your old lady."

"She's in my fuckin' house, isn't she?" Bear was livid. That much was certain. This was a side of the man I never wanted focused on me. "Be very fuckin' glad I'm not the one to decide what happens to you. Not only did you disrespect my woman, but you pulled a fuckin' knife on me."

"It was reflex, Bear. I swear I wasn't gonna use it!"

"Don't care. Get the fuck out."

"Come on, Wood." Banjo took hold of his arm and led the man outside. French took the knife and laid it on a table by the couch. He glanced up at Bear before the three of them left. Banjo snagged the trash bag on his way out.

Bear carefully removed the dish towel from my arm. The cut wasn't deep, but it was long. It still oozed blood, but it wasn't bad. He wrapped it tight around my arm again before picking up his phone and shooting off a text.

"Gonna get Bullet to come look at this. At the very least you'll need a tetanus shot."

"Why would you care?" I was trying very hard to keep from breaking down. My heart pounded, and my arm was starting to sting like a motherfucker.

"You heard me claim you, Liv. That means you're mine to protect. That means I beat a fuckin' prospect for being disrespectful, that's what I do. You hurt yourself? I get you a doctor. Which brings up my first question. What the fuck were you doing?"

"I was trying to keep you from getting stabbed," I snapped. Taking a deep breath, I closed my eyes. The adrenaline was leaving my body, and I was shaky and nauseous. I tried to turn around to wash my hands, but my knees chose that moment to buckle and I thought I was going to hit the floor. Instead, Bear's strong arms came around me, pulling me solidly against his muscled body.

"Careful, honey."

My hands landed on his chest as I looked up into his eyes. Instead of the feral look of a few minutes ago when he was strangling the man who'd made a crude comment to me, he now wore an expression of concern.

"Bear?" My breathing quickened and I moistened my lips.

"Christ, woman," he growled in a husky voice. "Don't do that unless you want me to kiss you. Because I can't think of doing anything else."

A little whimper escaped me just before Bear lowered his lips to mine and took my mouth in a tender but firm kiss.

Warmth swept through my body, a heat from within as I surrendered to Bear's kiss.

Bear's lips were rough and demanding but gentle as they moved against mine, claiming and possessing. There was a wild, woodsy taste to him, strong and intoxicating. I permitted him access when he gently nudged my lips apart with his tongue, exploring every inch of my mouth. I moaned softly into the kiss, my hand fisting in his shirt. His free hand moved up my back to cradle the back of my head, holding me closer to him as if he was afraid I might slip away.

My knees finally gave out, and Bear had my full weight. He bent and picked me up, one arm under my ass. I wrapped my legs around him automatically and he grunted his approval. He never let up on the kiss, taking my mouth in a sensual and lust filled act that threatened to make me lose my mind.

There was a knock at the door and Bear growled into my mouth. He didn't stop either. Just kept thrusting his tongue inside my mouth to flick and taste.

When the knock came again and a man called out, "Bear? Wanna let me in?" Bear groaned and ended the kiss. He pressed his forehead to mine, his breathing as ragged as my own.

"Christ," he muttered. "Wait here, Liv. It's Bullet. Do not get down. Understand?" He pinned me with a firm gaze.

I nodded, unable to actually form even a word as simple as "yes." He patted my thigh and leaned back down to kiss my forehead, then went to the door to let in the other man.

I wanted to jump down and bolt. Run to a room in the house and barricade myself inside where no one could get me. Except I totally believed Bear when he'd told me before he'd break down any door between us. Having seen the way he moved when Redwood spoke to me, I knew he was capable of violence. Hadn't I been warned by Black these men were dangerous? I was still trying to reconcile a man who could help slaughter a village of innocent people with the man with me now. Not only was he gentle with me, but he'd assaulted a member of his own club, a man he presumably knew much better than he did me, on my behalf.

Not for the first time, I started to question what I'd been told about these people. What if Black had been lying? Lord knew he'd lied about plenty since the first time I'd met him. The pressure inside me was mounting by the second. This wasn't me. I wasn't a spy or soldier. I was just a girl afraid to break away from a father she knew had put her in this situation to begin with simply because he was her family. You stuck by family. Supported them. Right? But how could I betray people who'd taken me in with no questions asked simply because I'd said I was in trouble and needed help? The questions had only come after they'd gotten me safely away from the situation.

So my dilemma now became whether or not to continue with my instructions, or take a leap of faith and tell Bear everything. Let him help me figure out what to do. Assuming he was even interested.

This was something I really needed to think about, but I didn't have a lot of time. One thing was certain, though. This thing was becoming less and less about helping my father and more about being able to look myself in the mirror after it was done. When I believed they were essentially mass murderers, it was easier. I wasn't going to be the one to harm them. I'd believed they'd done some truly horrible things.

Now? Yeah. I needed some time to sort this out. Because my gut was telling me this situation wasn't black-and-white. There were a million shades of gray. I wasn't remotely qualified for the sort of task I'd been given. Betraying these people would not only be the wrong thing to do, but it could destroy my soul.

Chapter Six

Bear

Going postal on Redwood hadn't been intentional. Yeah, the little punk deserved what I'd dished out and more, and yeah, I'd meant it. No one in this club was touching or even thinking about touching Olivia. Which was a huge problem for me while she hadn't yet told me the truth about what the fuck was going on with her.

Bullet cleaned her wound, putting a bandage over it after he washed off the blood drying on her skin as well as the fresh seepage. "I think a few Steri-Strips'll do. Put a bandage on it until it completely stops bleeding, but you won't need to keep it on long if you don't want to. When was your last tetanus shot?"

"I-I don't really remember?" Olivia darted a brief glance at me before looking back down at her lap. She sat at the dining table while Bullet taped her wound together. He grunted, putting a small dressing over the wound before sitting back and studying her. "I'll get you a tetanus shot and some antibiotics. You allergic to anything?"

"No."

"Good. I'll be right back." He smiled at Olivia, then stood to leave. "I'd have brought it with me, but I was closer to here than I was my office when you messaged." He hiked his thumb over his shoulder at the door. "Saw Banjo, Redwood, and French on the way out." When I didn't say anything, he continued. "None of 'em looked too happy." Still, I said nothing. Bullet sighed. "OK, then. Nice chat. I'll be right back."

I grunted and turned back to Olivia. Bullet could show his own fucking self out the fucking door. Olivia kept her gaze lowered, twisting her fingers together. I stood there right in front of her for a long while. She kept her gaze down but darting around the room as if looking for an escape.

"Olivia..." I sighed, scrubbing my hand over my face. "Honey, why would you do that? Put yourself between two men who are more than twice your size? He could have accidentally hurt you."

"You could have hurt me too."

"Honey, no matter what's going on or how upset I get, there is no situation where I *accidentally* hurt you."

"Meaning, if you hurt me, it's intentional."

Something strange unfurled inside me. I immediately knew she was wrong. I couldn't imagine a situation where I ever hurt her intentionally, even if I wanted to. Wasn't altogether sure I could even if I *had* to. Or was ordered to. So I decided if I wanted her to be honest with me, I needed to be honest with her. If that meant I admitted how attracted I was to her, I'd lay it out there for her.

"Meaning, anything I do to cause you pain will ultimately give you pleasure. And it won't be accidental. It will be deliberate and premeditated. And you'll beg me for it."

Olivia sucked in a breath. Her gaze snapped up to mine, and one hand landed lightly on my chest before she snatched it away. "Sorry," she whispered.

I shifted my weight so I inched closer to her. Slowly, I reached down and took her hand, bringing it back to my chest. I held it there, letting her feel my heartbeat through my shirt. "Touch me if you want," I murmured. "Might as well get used to me now. You're gonna be touchin' me a lot in the future. Same as I'll be touchin' you."

"I-I c-can't."

"I told you the truth about the only pain I'd ever bring to you. Now, I want your truth. You said you had a boyfriend. Do you?"

She opened her mouth, then swallowed. This time, when she spoke, I knew she was telling the truth. "No." Her confirmation was a breathy whisper, one that wrapped around my heart and squeezed. To say nothing of what it did to my cock.

"See? That wasn't so hard. Was it?"

"Why are you doing this? I know you don't trust me."

I didn't hesitate in my answer. "No, Liv. I don't. But you're going to tell me what's going on. Then I'm gonna take care of whatever trouble's found you. Once that's done, we can get on with learning to trust each other."

The expressions on her face changed rapidly. I saw surprise, hope, disappointment. Sadness. Then a steely resolve. Olivia shook her head. "No. That will never happen."

"Which part? Because there's a lot of stuff I intend to do."

"All of it!" She sidestepped to get around me, then crossed the room. She was deeper inside my home, but too fucking far away from me for my liking. Only thing that kept me from moving back to her was the fact she had nowhere to go and couldn't get out of the house without me being able to stop her. "Bear, just..." She sobbed in a shuddering breath. "Please. Give me my phone back and let me go home," she finished with a little whimper.

"Sorry, darlin'. Can't until this is all straightened out. Crush is checkin' your phone out. Once he's satisfied it's secure, he'll get it back to you."

"I can't stay here, Bear. I can't."

"Tell me why."

"It's not that simple."

"Sure it is. Only thing missin's trust. As in you don't trust me, so you've not told me the truth. You not tellin' me what's goin' on makes me not trust you."

"And I have to trust you to tell you so we're back at the beginning." She sounded equal parts exasperated and almost desperate. "I don't know what to do!" she yelled at me, tears starting to stream down her face. "If I don't tell you and something happens, I'm dead. If I tell you and you can't protect me, I'm worse than dead! Like you said, there isn't a scenario where this ends well for me!"

This was my opening. She wanted to tell me; it was easy to see. She'd given me just that little bit of an opening, and I knew I had to take it. I crossed the room, taking back the distance she'd put between us. "Listen to me, baby, and listen hard. I claimed you as mine. In the eyes of the club, you're just as important as me. Maybe more so because you're a woman. Grim Road is many things. Most of them not good. But we do not prey on the weak. We don't subjugate our women. The club whores are here for one purpose. They know what's expected of them before they come here. They still have the right to say no, and they can leave any time they want."

Her eyes widened and her lips parted. I could tell that, for whatever reason, I'd shocked her.

"All the women with us could be in danger just by associating with us. We accept responsibility for that and don't take the danger to them lightly. We protect them. The women protect the children. We all protect each other." I gave her my hardest stare. The one that said I meant every fucking word I was saying and had the means, motive, and opportunity to follow through with my promise. "You're already mine, Liv. I claimed you. Told them you're mine. That means every single man in this clubhouse will protect you with his life. Same as he would for all the women. You're ours, and we're all family. We protect our family."

It was either the exact right thing or the exact wrong thing to say. Either way, Olivia dissolved into tears. She took in great gulps of air only to continue to sob as she sank to the floor in a small heap.

I crossed the distance to her in slow, careful steps. The last thing I wanted to do was spook her. I wanted her to feel safe with me. Then, maybe she'd tell me what the shit was going on, and I could take care of it for her.

When I reached her, I crouched down in front of her, taking her hand in mine. "Honey, talk to me. Tell me what's going on."

She sniffed, wiping her nose on the back of her wrist. I stood and got her a paper towel, letting her clean up while I went to the bathroom and got a wet washcloth. When I got back, she was rocking back and forth slightly, like a child trying to comfort herself.

I sat beside her, putting my arm around her and raising the cloth to her face to gently wipe the tear stains away. I felt her body shivering where we touched. When she looked up into my eyes there was a quiet resignation I hated. She was terrified. At the end of her rope with no idea what to do next. I willed her to take a leap of faith and give this to me. I'd take care of it and prove I could be a worthy protector.

She looked down at her hands, twisting the paper towel in her hand. "I'm supposed to..." She swallowed, closing her eyes tightly. "Spy. On the club." Before I could say anything, she continued rapidly. Like she needed to get it out before she changed her mind. "I was supposed to activate an app on the phone they gave me and they'd do the rest. I have no idea what it does exactly, but I think it somehow lets them into anything connected to the Internet or a cell service or something."

"Who's 'they', Liv?"

"I only know him as Mr. Black. He was one of the guys who chased me to you and Ringo. He's an associate of my father."

The relief I felt was instant. She was telling the truth. Sure, I already knew this, but it was a step in the right direction. Maybe she was going to take the leap of faith after all. "Good, Olivia. That's good. Do you know what he and your father do to help each other?"

She shook her head. "I'll tell you everything I know." She raised her head to meet my gaze with her own. She looked haunted. Terrified. "But you have to understand, I tried my best to keep my head down and not notice anything."

"Just tell me what you know, and the club will take care of the rest."

"My father is an international businessman. At least, that's what he wants everyone to believe. What he really does is inform for the CIA."

"Where?"

"You mean, what country? City?" When I nodded, she continued. "A lot of places. I'm not sure of the exact places, but I can tell you he has offices in Berlin, Dubai, Tripoli, Cairo... He's even got offices in Moscow and St. Petersburg. All of it is a front. Oh, he makes money. Hand over fist. But it's not his natural gas company or even the companies he owns under the table taking in all that money to clean up the Chernobyl site."

"A front for what?"

She shrugged, shaking her head and looking about as miserable as a person could. "I swear I don't know. All I know is Mr. Black is an integral part of it all. I know there are places they're trying to clear out. Small places where no one will care."

"Clear out?" Though I knew what she meant, I wanted to see how much she actually knew.

Fresh tears filled her eyes and spilled down her cheeks as she started sobbing again. "I'm sure I don't know the half of it, but I've heard them talking. Once I had to go with him to Tripoli. The day we left to come home there was a news report about a village not a hundred miles to the south that had been destroyed. The images looked like some kind of bomb had gone off. But the really horrible part was, there had been people who survived only to be shot as they fled. I heard Mr. Black and my father toasting 'finally wiping that shithole off the map so we can make some fucking money.' Their words. Not mine."

"Did he tell you why he wanted you to spy on us?"

"He said he had a job for you, Bear. You by name. He said if I got caught, I was to tell you he had you by the balls and that you better do your fucking job this time."

"He say how he had me by the balls? What he was holding over me and what he expected to happen?"

"Pretty sure he thought he was going to find something when I infiltrated this place and turned on that app. As to what he had planned, I don't know for sure, but the target's in the mountains of Afghanistan. I'm just not sure what or exactly where. I got the impression that, just like that town south of Tripoli, this was a small group, probably sitting on something the CIA wants and are unwilling or unable to negotiate for. They said it was very remote and no one would miss the place, but they don't want to leave any evidence behind, so he's looking for a professional cleaning crew. He said that's what you used to do, Bear. You cleaned an area and left no trace. Not like the mess they had back in Tripoli."

If she believed Leon Black when he'd told her I'd eliminated entire villages just because someone told me to, I could understand her hesitation to trust me.

"Telling me this took courage. I'm proud of you for taking a chance and trusting me." I smiled down at her. "Thank you, Olivia."

She looked up at me with wide, brown eyes. "Are you going to hurt me? If you are, I can take it. I just can't take not knowing." She ended on a little sob before swallowing loudly to get her emotions under control. I had no doubt she was terrified. Any woman in her position would be, and she'd be smart to be scared.

"Already told you, honey." I grinned down at her, stroking her jaw gently with my finger. "I'll never hurt you unless you ask me to, and only with pleasure being the end result." I winked at her, trying to lighten the mood and help her be at ease when she was anything but.

"What about your president or vice president? The other men in Grim Road?"

"Not lettin' anyone hurt you. Is there anything else I need to know? I know Venus searched you. You told me about your phone. Is there anything else you need to tell me. Anything at all? Even if it's just bits and pieces."

"No."

"What made you change your mind about telling

me, Liv?" I needed to know this most of all. I knew we still had a long way to go to trust each other, but I thought she might have the same instinctive pull toward me as I did her.

"You guys might be a lot of things, but you're not the kind of men to kill innocent people, let alone commit some kind of genocide. I wanted to believe you when you first picked me up and put me on your bike." Pink tinged her cheeks, and I knew she was uncomfortable. Embarrassed or nervous, maybe. But I thought it was more than that. "And the second I jumped into your arms, something inside me settled. I felt safe for the first time in a long time. I want that feeling for the rest of my life. I tried to justify what Mr. Black wanted me to do with the fact that you were murderers. That you'd killed innocent women and children because you were being paid to. I thought I could deny the blood on my hands because I wouldn't be the one to pull the trigger. But that was a lame justification. I'm not sure I could have gone through with it even if I still believed you were murderers, but after the way you treated me, how you protected me and never demanded anything, not even immediate answers, until you had me in a safe place. Those aren't the actions of cold-blooded killers. At least not someone who could kill innocent people for money."

I grinned. "I'll take it, honey. Now. You OK?"

She nodded. "I think so. What do I do now? Crush didn't turn on the phone here, did he? Because I don't trust Mr. Black or anything he gives me. Just connecting to the network could be bad."

"No. He took it somewhere else where he said he'd have more control over everything."

"Good." She whispered her response and ducked her head again. "Bear?" She didn't look up.

"Yeah, baby."

"I'm really sorry I intended to betray you."

"You didn't know me. Still don't, but you know the important things."

She nodded. "Yeah."

"But just so you know I'll do my best to never keep anything from you or mislead you, when I was in the Middle East, my team was assigned to that same fuckin' village near Tripoli. When we got there, we were given the order that the place was to be... liquidated. No one was to survive to be able to give an account of what happened."

She sucked in a breath. "Oh no..." I could see the fear and horror in her face as my words really sank in.

"Yeah. But I refused the order. We worked for the CIA, doing their dirty work. That village was too much, though. I wasn't about to slaughter those people."

"You promise? I mean, you're telling me the truth. Right?"

"I am. That mission is how I ended up here at Grim Road. Rocket took me in and let me disappear. Everyone here has been in some form of Black Ops. We've all done some horrible things. But none of us would do that. Black tried to come after me. Tried to kill me more than once before I finally made it here. After that, Crush took over, and I disappeared."

Olivia sagged against me. I don't know if it was relief or if the adrenaline rush left her, but she looked exhausted. "OK. So, from this point forward, I'll trust you. Bear, please don't make me regret it. And I don't mean that as a threat. I mean, you're right. I want this thing with you. You claiming me, or whatever. I think I crave that sense of safety you give me because I'm willing to risk my life for this. Because, if it's real, then

I'll have everything I've ever wanted in a man. If it's not, then I'm no worse off than I was."

"I swear to you, honey. You'll always be safe. From now as long as anyone in Grim Road is around. I will always protect you."

"All right, then." She gave me a solemn look. "What happens now?"

"Tonight? You sleep. I'll sleep with you if you want, but only to help you feel safe. Nothing physical is happening tonight."

The look on her face said that surprised her. "You don't want to... uh... have sex with me?"

"Oh, make no mistake. I very much want to have sex with you. But you're not ready. And I'm not taking advantage of you. You are going to be with me as much as possible, and you're gonna sleep in my bed with me. You need to get used to my touch, and I just fuckin' want you in my arms."

Surprisingly, that got a nervous laugh from her. "Never slept next to a man before. I might kick."

I gave her my best wicked grin. "Good. I like my woman to have a bit of spirit."

That got a better laugh, and she actually smiled. And, God, I was so fucked. The girl was absolutely gorgeous. That fucking smile was fucking breathtaking.

There was no way I was getting out of this with my man card intact. Because I was already pussy-whipped. I'd follow this girl wherever the fuck she wanted to go. And Goddamn the consequences.

Chapter Seven

Olivia

I drifted in sleep, somewhere close to awake but with this soft, hazy cocoon around my mind. And my body? I stretched and rolled over...

And my pillow moved. Only it wasn't a pillow. It was a big, strong arm. Then that arm was joined by another muscled one wrapping around me and pulling me closer. A decidedly male groan settled around me as he shifted under me until I lay with my head on his shoulder, his arms solidly around me.

"Bear?" He grunted. It was still full dark. It had been late when he'd lain down with me. "What time is it?" Seemed like an inane thing to say, but what did one say in a situation like this? I'd never slept with a guy before.

Instead of answering, he grunted again, rolling more fully onto his back and taking me with him. I sucked in a breath when he maneuvered me on top of him, settling me so that I straddled him.

I had no idea what I was supposed to do. His breathing evened out, but his grip on me didn't relax. Or maybe his arms were just that heavy.

What was I supposed to do now? I kind of needed to pee, but would he get mad if I tried to move or woke him up? And, honestly, did I really want to move? The longer I stayed there, the more relaxed I got...

Until, I felt his cock stirring beneath me. I must have whimpered because Bear's arms tightened around me, and he nuzzled the top of my head with his chin. He didn't say anything and I wasn't sure he was actually awake. When I didn't move, he grunted again before his breathing evened out once more.

I was still for a minute, not really sure what to do. Then something inside me bubbled up and I wanted to giggle. Why? Not sure. I thought I might be losing my mind, but for some reason I wasn't actually scared. It was more like it was a relief to not be worried about when things were all going to go south. I didn't make a sound, but my body kept tensing up with the need to laugh.

"Don't see anything so Goddamned funny," Bear mumbled from beneath me. He sounded put out and adorably cranky, but I refrained from saying so. Also, the way he rubbed my back and brushed his chin over my head, his beard catching in my hair, put me at ease. Like he was soothing me through the gruff way he spoke. I took that as my permission to go ahead and chuckle.

"I'm sorry," I said as I let out some of the emotions I'd been carrying around. "Honest. I'm not laughing at you."

"That so? Then who you laughin' at?"

I sighed, stretching again. His cock was now at full attention, rubbing along my clit with every movement I made. Trying to ignore it was beyond difficult. "Not laughing at anyone. Just... laughing."

He grunted again. This time, he moved one hand to rub my back in soothing circles while he held me. "At least you ain't cryin'. Don't like that."

That settled the laughter, but not in a bad way. It just brought everything into perspective. "I'm still not certain this is going to work, Bear."

"What? You and me?"

"Yeah. I don't know you. You don't know me. I'm essentially a spy. Your club's not going to be OK with this. Especially once your tech guy gets into that phone."

"That was before. I laid it all out for Rocket and Lemon. Lemon is solidly in your corner. Rocket is reserving judgment because he believes you came clean because of that phone."

I sighed. "I mean, he's not wrong. Not entirely. Though, the phone wasn't the only reason."

"Honey, you asked for your phone *once*. Right before you told me what was going on. And I'm pretty sure it was a half-hearted attempt at best."

"Well, you weren't letting me go. I knew that."

Bear continued to make lazy strokes up and down my back with his big hand. It was so soothing. Comforting in a way I'd rarely known in my life. Was I so starved for affection that even a man I didn't know could make me putty in his hands simply by being nice to me?

No. It was more than that. He'd rescued me without question and stayed with me after, even knowing there was something not right.

I took a breath and pushed myself up so that I could look down at Bear. His cock pulsed and I couldn't suppress the gasp of surprise and pleasure. His cock moved against my clit every time it throbbed.

"You want my kiss?" God, could a man's voice sound any sexier? There was a deep rumble in his chest that vibrated my insides in the most erotic way.

"I shouldn't."

He grinned. "Probably not. Gonna take it anyway?"

"Like I could resist." The second the words were out of my mouth, his lips found mine. I couldn't help it. I surrendered to Bear, knowing there was no way to keep my heart out of this, no matter how much I needed to.

His lips were warm and hard, demanding and

consuming. His hands went from soothing me to gripping my ass, lifting me against him. I gasped into his mouth as he angled his hips so that his cock was aligned perfectly with my pussy. He scraped over my clit through our clothing sending electric fire straight through me. His size... simply to God couldn't be right. Bear was a massive man, but surely he wasn't as big as he felt. If so, he was massive in all respects. Bigger than anything I'd ever taken before. I shuddered at the thought of him inside me, stretching me until I was useless when he was done. Because I knew in my heart he'd make me enjoy it. And I'd never want another man other than Bear as long as I lived.

I must have stiffened at the thought because Bear pulled back and looked at me then. "We can stop any time you want. I want this, Liv, but not at the expense of your trust."

I nodded several times. I didn't know what to do. "I want you to, but..."

"You're scared?"

Tears came again even as I leaned in and kissed him again. The feel of his lips was a soothing balm to my every worry and fear. To lose myself in this man, even for a little while, would be the best bliss...

I cupped his face, his beard slightly coarse against my palm. He was so unlike men I knew. My sexual experience was limited, but I'd always been with refined men. Men my father approved of. My father would never approve of Bear. That thought spurred me on.

"Only what happens, you know. After."

"After? After I fuck you into oblivion?" That gruff, rusty voice of his sent shivers through me, and my nipples peaked, my pussy wept. "After that, you really will be mine. No going back for either of us."

"Because your club won't let us?" I wasn't sure I liked the sound of that. I didn't want any man to be trapped because of me. I also wasn't sure I could take it if he casually moved on afterward.

"Because I've never claimed a woman. Not for any reason. I already had no intentions of letting you go, but once I fuck you, that's it."

"That's crazy." My denial sounded as breathless as I felt. "But if you're trying to make sex with you unappealing, I have to tell you, it's not working."

He flashed me a sexy smirk. "You like the thought of belonging to me. Don't you?"

"Maybe. But only in fantasy. Belonging to someone in reality is never as good as it sounds."

"Sounds like you're talkin' from experience." He frowned down at me, but didn't let me go. In fact, he rolled over to pin me between him and the mattress, letting me take his weight. It was a delicious feeling I shouldn't have enjoyed but did.

"My father's a very wealthy man, Bear. He got that way by controlling everyone around him. That includes me." It hurt to make the admission, and I'm sure I winced.

"Everyone except Leon Black."

"Yeah. Which is how I ended up here."

"You regret being here?" He raised an eyebrow, but I could see he really wanted the answer.

"I regret the reason for it. But not that I met you. I just wish it were under different circumstances." I stroked the side of his face, and he leaned into my touch before turning his head and kissing my palm.

"Everything happens for a reason, Liv. Even bad things. Perhaps a bad thing brought you to me, but you're here. Now. Be honest with me and everything else will work itself out. I want you."

I took a deep breath and nodded. "Okay, but no regrets."

"None from me." He growled before deepening the kiss. His large frame was heavy and imposing. I loved the feel of his weight pinning me. Loved it more than I ever imagined I would. Instead of feeling trapped, all I felt was joy. Life. Excitement. And a lust so deep it bordered on obsession.

"Now, it's me and you, Olivia. Nothing else exists. All right?" he asked as he held his weight with his forearms next to my head. His fingers played in the hair around my face as he gentled me beneath his touch.

"What about your club? You have to be with Grim Road."

"Honey, I'll always be with Grim. This is my home. But the members of Grim don't accept you, you're still my choice. I get the final say on what woman I take. And I'll always protect you. From everything and everyone."

He kissed me again, this time harder, coaxing me to open for him. I did so willingly and moaned as Bear plundered my mouth. He tasted of sin and that niggle of fear I'd had for him before raced through me again, but this time it was accompanied by a healthy dose of arousal.

"Last chance, baby." He licked my neck, then kissed his way from my lips to my cheek, and down my neck. His words were muffled against my skin and the material of my shirt.

"I want this," I whispered. "I want to know what it feels like. To be yours."

"Good." Bear sat up, his thighs firmly between mine. My legs draped over his legs as he sat back on his heels and peeled off his shirt. His muscled, tattooed chest, shoulders, and arms were magnificent.

He undid his pants, and his cock sprang free. No underwear. I blushed tomato red as he stared at me, as if daring me to change my mind. His member was thick and hard, and just the sight of him made my pussy ache for him.

"God, you're beautiful." I breathed out the words, before covering my mouth with my hand.

He chuckled and tugged it away with a teasing growl. "You're gonna like this. I promise."

Bear set about removing my shirt, his mouth hot on my skin as he bared me inch by inch. He moaned in appreciation, before running his devilishly skilled fingers over first one breast, then the other. He took his time, caressing me everywhere except where I needed it most.

"Bear." I whined as he unfastened my pants. He grinned down at me as he peeled them off my legs, panties and all, and tossed them to the floor. Then he cupped my pussy possessively with his large hand. I moaned, tilting my hips toward him and arching my back. "Oh, my God!" The words came out a breathy whimper.

He chuckled. "You can call me Bear, sweetheart."

When I laughed, he took advantage, opening his mouth and planting it against my neck. The slight stinging against my skin told me he'd marked me. It also tickled like shit, and I squealed with laughter. "Stop!" I thrashed as I laughed, trying to get away from the sensation even as my pussy wept.

"Wee bit ticklish, are you?"

"Bear!"

He didn't let up, though. Instead, he slid down my body, his beard abrading the skin of my chest and abdomen. When he reached the skin just below my belly button, he gave a sharp nip with his teeth that had me yelping. He just chuckled as he continued downward.

"Gonna eat you up, baby." Then Bear took a long, slow lick through my folds, flicking my clit at the end.

This time, I screamed. My thighs clamped around his head before I realized it. Bear didn't seem to mind, though. His tongue licked and flicked while his mouth sucked and nipped. The sensations were too much. Before I even realized I was on the verge, I came in a wet rush, screaming his name as I tunneled my fingers through his hair to hold him to me even tighter.

My head spun and my heart pounded. I squeezed my eyes shut as the waves of my orgasm continued to crash over me with brutal intensity.

The next thing I knew, Bear was over me. I could feel his cock poking at my entrance. I felt the latex barrier between us and knew he'd used protection.

In one smooth motion, Bear entered me, stretching me with his girth. I gasped at the invasion, which he only met with a kiss, all cocky confidence and arrogance. He felt so good inside me, filling me up like I'd been made for him.

"Damn, baby," he moaned into my mouth as he began to move. "You feel so fucking good."

Bear moved with a steady rhythm, bringing me to the brink of another orgasm, only to pull back. My nails dug into his back, trying to urge him on faster.

"Greedy, huh?" He chuckled, but sped his thrusts just the same.

"Never..." I swallowed, shaking my head slightly and closing my eyes tight for a brief moment. I needed to get myself under control. The last thing I wanted was to look as inexperienced as I really was. I wasn't a virgin, but my sexual encounters had been extremely limited and never with a man like this. "Never felt anything like this. Please!" I begged.

Bear grinned as he slid out of me with an exaggerated slowness that almost had me growling.

"Bear," I gasped, arching upward. "What are you doing to me?" I was desperate. All thoughts of trying to hold my reactions in check went out the door the third time he let me fall back down without cresting that wave of pleasure threatening to drown me.

He groaned into my neck. "Ride me, then, baby. Let me feel you come on my cock. Now!"

Oh, God, those dirty words. I moaned and began to rock my hips, meeting him thrust for thrust. He was so big and hard inside me. The friction between us caused a slow burn as I once again spiraled out of control. "Bear!"

"Fuck, yes," he growled into my ear. His hips pounded against mine, slamming us both into the mattress.

I screamed as the pleasure built to dizzying heights. My nails raked down his back, digging into his skin while my body convulsed under him.

The bed frame creaked under our combined weight and frantic motions. My back arched as I rode him higher and higher, my nails sinking into his rock-hard abs. "AHH!" I screamed as I came apart around him.

Bear growled and tensed, burying himself to the hilt inside me as he joined me with his own climax.

We lay there, panting and sweaty. Bear had his face buried in my neck, kissing and murmuring softly to me as I came down from the orgasmic high. My heart still pounded in my chest but was gradually slowing to a more sedate level.

"That's it, pretty girl," he murmured. "Fuckin' beautiful."

As my vision cleared, I noticed my fingernails were still embedded in one shoulder and his back. "Oh, shit!" I let go, pulling my arms away and looking up at him with what was probably horror on my face. "I'm so sorry!"

Bear burst out laughing, burying his face back in my neck. His beard tickled my fevered skin so that I squirmed beneath him, instinctively trying to get away. Which would have been pretty hard, considering he was still firmly imbedded inside me.

"Easy there, baby." He chuckled, still licking and sucking at my skin.

"I scratched you."

"Yep. You sure did, baby." He didn't sound the least bit upset. "Pretty sure you drew blood."

"Oh no…" I was shocked, but the orgasmic high wouldn't leave me. It felt almost satisfying to know I'd marked him. Which wasn't a good thing.

"Don't sound so horrified. You marked me as yours. I'm good with that."

"Did I hurt you?" I peeked up at him, dreading that I'd see anger or irritation on his face.

"Honey, the day a little pipsqueak like you hurts me is the day I turn in my man card." He rolled us so that I lay sprawled on top of him. His dick was still in my pussy. "Now kiss me and we'll go clean up."

Who was I to deny him? Especially when I wanted more of his kisses. I could easily become addicted to his kisses.

I expected him to set me on my feet and smack my ass as I headed to the bathroom or something, but instead, he sat up with me in his arms, my legs straddling his hips, and carried me to the bathroom and set me on the vanity.

He turned on the hot water and let it heat while retrieving a couple of washcloths and discarding the condom. He didn't take long and I just sat there. I was equal parts stunned and crashing. I'd just had the best sex I'd ever imagined, and there was still a possibility this man could turn into my worst enemy.

"If things go to shit later, Bear, I just want you to know that was one of the best experiences of my life."

For long moments, Bear said nothing. He did take the washcloth from my trembling fingers and gently cleaned me before tossing the cloth in the hamper. When he returned his attention back to me, he braced his hands on either side of my hips and held my gaze with his for several moments.

Finally, he sighed. "Honey, even if things go to shit later, I'm still on your side until you prove to me you're not on mine. I'm here to protect you. I'm gonna keep you safe from my enemies. You're going to be as much a part of this club as the other women. They'll support you. I'll support you."

"These guys, Bear…" I cringed away, shaking my head. "They're bad news. They said they are CIA, but if they are, they're not operating inside the agency. At least, I hope they're not. If our government does this kind of thing to people inside their own country, I'm not sure how anyone could support them."

"Do you know what the end goal is?"

"All I know is they want to, in their words, 'take down that whole motherfucking club and put them in their place.' That's a direct quote. I recorded it on my real cell phone. The one at home in my room. They wouldn't let me take it because they said two phones would be suspicious enough for them to not let me in."

"So, we have the guys make a run for your house

and steal it." He shrugged as though it was no big deal.

"You say that like it's easy. My father has top-notch security. Government level. I'm not sure you understood the 'international businessman' part of what he does. He's a billionaire, Bear. You're not going to just break in and take what you want."

"You know what they have on your father? Why they'd turn on him if he's giving them valuable information, which, with those kinds of connections with the very wealthy of the world, he's probably giving them some pretty damned good shit."

"Something to do with money. I think they threatened to tell some of his contacts he'd been siphoning money from them or something. And no, I don't know who or how or anything else. That was all I learned before they caught me. Just some vague notion of what was going on so I wouldn't put much stock in it."

"Good to know. Now, I need to go plan this thing with Rocket. We'll get your personal phone and let Crush and Byte take over."

"You don't have to go get my phone, Bear. I can access it from the cloud."

He blinked at me. "I beg your pardon?"

I blinked right back at him. "The cloud? Cyber storage? As in, uploaded to...?" He gave me a blank look that was also a dare for me to laugh, grin, or in any other way make fun of how old he was. I cleared my throat. "All right, then. How about you tell Crush. Sounds like he'll know what to do from there."

He gave me a disgruntled look. "I think I'm way the fuck too old for you."

I gave him a fierce scowl, hoping like hell he thought I was teasing when I kind of really meant what I was about to say. "Doesn't matter if you are or not.

No take-backs. It's a rule."

That got him. He must have not been expecting me to say something like that because he let out a belly laugh before wrapping his arms tightly around me as he continued to chuckle. "No way, baby. No take-backs. I swear."

Chapter Eight

Bear

"Well, she was right about one thing. If she'd managed to activate this application, whoever controls this thing would have been able to control every piece of electronic equipment we have connected to the network." Crush had basically come back to the compound bare-ass naked and without the phone. "I took care of it but, I gotta tell ya, I'd love to get my hands on that tech for us."

"What'd you do with it?"

Crush shrugged. "Buried it. Once I find out where it came from, I'll figure out what to do next."

"We didn't dare even bring the thing near the compound." Byte picked up the explanation. "Even with the battery out and the whole thing taken apart, we weren't sure if it was safe." He shook his head. "Didn't want that thing anywhere near us. Crush didn't even use his burner phone to call me after being in close proximity to her phone."

"This something normal with spooks today?"

Crush tilted his head. "I wouldn't say normal. There are several devices I'm aware of that *might* do something similar, but not to this degree. It was hard to figure out, but once that thing is on, there's no guarantee I could prevent it from..." He paused and shook his head slightly, like he couldn't believe what he was about to say. "I was in a relatively rural area when I turned on the phone. Within seconds, I started getting data from every single phone on that particular cell tower and the two open Wi-Fi networks close to me. Just two houses in the neighborhood. But now, that phone has access to every one of those devices anytime it's connected to a public access network or cell tower and is able to receive data."

"Huh. That's pretty hard core. 'Course, it's the government." Ringo shrugged, obviously not impressed. "It didn't get in here. Olivia was searched thoroughly, her clothes replaced and everything she had with her left behind. Venus found the phone and didn't turn it on."

"No, but I'm replacing her phone anyway. Everyone who was near Olivia. Just in case. Any electronics that got anywhere near that thing needs replacing. Including the fuckin' cages." Crush grumbled. "This is gonna be a fuckin' nightmare. And, honestly, Rocket. If that phone picked up on any of the navigation systems, they already know where we are."

Rocket crossed his arms over his chest, studying Crush. "We'll figure that out later. Keep the damage as minimal as you can. If we have to replace the vehicles, we will."

"Already moved anything that might possibly have come near that phone to a section of the property well away from the compound. Thankfully, all but the ride you guys came in was still in town when I figured it out. So it's gonna take a while, but I can fix that."

"Next thing," Rocket continued. "What does the CIA want with us?"

"Olivia indicated they've got some kind of grudge against us," I said. "Want to put us in our place. She said she has proof." I handed Crush a piece of paper. "Olivia said that's her cloud account. Said the video she took from her phone is backed up there."

Crush and Byte looked at each other. The pair was creepy like that. They seemed to know what the other was thinking. "Could be more of the same technology," Crush muttered, not taking his gaze from his brother. "What do you think?"

"We can do it remotely. I've got a clean laptop I use for testing. I'll take it somewhere safe and check into it. Just to be safe, I'm not bringing it back for anyone here to see." Byte looked at Rocket. "You'll have to take my word for it."

Lemon waved him off. "Don't see why we need anything else. You say it's so, it's so. I'm more concerned about why she was chosen to be the one to hunt us down." Lemon's face could have been carved from granite. This was the vice president of Grim Road, determined to get to the bottom of the situation. It always amazed me how grown up she was. The woman was born for this life if anyone was. "Is there any way they've targeted Ringo or Bear in particular?"

"It's me," I said. "Leon Black is after me."

"He's a motherfucker of the first order," Rocket muttered. "I'd really hoped the world had seen the last of that prick."

"It's all because of the Tripoli incident." I shifted my feet. "Leon didn't get reprimanded or anything. He managed to put most of it off on me. But it cost him a high cabinet seat and possibly a bid for the White House. Not to mention he was in line for the directorship of the CIA and that went to shit immediately after."

"Makes sense he'd hold a grudge." Rocket rubbed his chin thoughtfully. "Happened on his watch, and they couldn't really do anything to you unless they found you. We took care of that."

"So, what now?" Lemon parked her ass against Rocket's desk, crossing her arms over her chest.

"Now," Rocket said, leaning in to kiss Lemon on the temple, "we hunt this guy down and let him know he's way the fuck out of bounds." He raised an eyebrow at me. "Your woman on board?"

"She's mine and knows it." I gave Rocket a level look. "She's probably gonna balk at severing ties with her father, but I think it needs doin'. He's part of the reason she's in this position in the first Goddamned place."

"Oh?"

"Apparently, Black and his bunch have something on the man. He's got some kind of international business with offices all over. Liv said Black threatened to expose him for stealin' money or something. She wasn't clear on the details. Only overheard part of the conversation."

"Do you trust her?" Bullet asked the question quietly. I knew my brother was only asking what needed to be asked.

"I've known her for a few hours, man. My mind is cautious, but my heart wants to believe her."

"You're in pretty fuckin' deep for as fast as this has happened, Bear. That's not like you." Ringo weighed in and, even though it irritated me, I knew he was right.

"If I could tell you why she calls to me on this kind of level I would, Ringo. I can't even explain it to myself, so I can't explain it to you. But Black is CIA. It's his business to know his people. Like it or not, I was once on his team."

"You think he sent her to you because he knew she was the type of woman you'd go for? Did he know you that well?" Rocket narrowed his eyes as he spoke, likely thinking really hard about the whole situation.

"You know the CIA as well or better than I do, Rocket. Those bastards know a man inside and out before they hire him. I was on Leon Black's team for three years. So, yeah. I have no doubt that bastard handpicked Olivia."

"And you're still claiming her?" Rocket looked frustrated. "Bear, you know I think you're the most capable man here. I'd trust you to have my back in any situation for any reason. But are you sure, really sure, about this?"

"I know it's crazy, Rocket. I know what's at stake. But she's mine. If she works against us, I'll accept responsibility. But I want her protected."

"If she stays in your corner, we will protect her to the death. You know that."

"I'm telling you right now, Rocket. I believe her. I believe she's told me what she knows and that she's the only innocent party in all this. God knows I'm not."

"You know what?" Lemon stood up straight then. "Crush. Where is this fucker?"

"Roadside motel. Other side of town. Him and the other guy." Crush met my gaze. "Goes by Boon."

That surprised me. "Boon? Paul Jacobs?"

"He was on that same team when you were in Tripoli, wasn't he?" Rocket raised a questioning eyebrow at me.

"Yeah." I scrubbed a hand over my face. "Christ, Rocket. Boon was the only man in that group who questioned our orders. The others were ready to go, but Boon stayed with me. I told him I could help him get out if he wanted to, but Boon had a family. He didn't want to uproot them. I have no idea what happened to him after I came here, but that whole unit was reprimanded. We weren't active military, so the CIA was able to keep it interagency." I shrugged. "They protected their men in the long term, but short term, it was a fuckin' shit show."

"Yeah," Crush confirmed. "He took the brunt of it all. Probably because he backed you up. Me and Rocket kept you out of the loop because you had enough on your plate, but Boon spent some time in prison because of that incident. He took the fall for them."

"Are you fuckin' kiddin' me?" I paced across the room. "Christ, Rocket! Why would you keep that from me?" For the first time since I'd known Rocket, I felt a sense of betrayal even as I knew he'd probably been right to keep me out of it.

"You were injured, comin' off that mission, knowin' you hadn't been able to stop a massacre. Your head wasn't in a good place, and I wasn't about to make it worse."

"I could have helped. Maybe kept him out of jail."

"Oh, really?" This from Lemon. "How could you have done that?"

"By testifyin' he wasn't there. That he was with me." The second I said it, I knew how utterly stupid I sounded.

"Right," Lemon continued, not pulling any punches. "The CIA is gonna believe you, a man who disobeyed orders and vanished off the face of the earth, over the man who was expecting to be the director of the CIA?" She snorted. "Honey, you ain't that convincin'."

I glared at my vice president. Rocket sighed. "Lemon, you don't have to be so fuckin' blunt."

"Ah. My mistake. I'll pussyfoot around it, put some sugar on it, and tell him the exact same fuckin' thing. Don't change the message. Bear is many things, but he's not a fuckin' pussy. He needs it raw and unfiltered to get through his thick skull."

Despite the gravity of the situation, I couldn't help but chuckle a little. "Don't listen to him, Lemon. You keep givin' it to us straight. Keep us honest."

She lifted her chin. "It's part of why you guys voted me in. I know it hurt, Bear. I know you don't like it." She turned to her man then. "But Bear's also right, Rocket. You should have told him. He had the right to know. The other men in Grim could have kept him here or helped him figure out a way to help Boon if he insisted."

Rocket glared at Lemon. "You're not helpin'."

"And you know I'm right." She pointed a finger at him, poking him in the chest. "So the question now is, what do we do about this Leon Black guy?"

Ringo shrugged. "He wants to talk to us? I say we give him what he wants."

* * *

Olivia

"I think I should go with you."

Bear told me the club planned to nab Mr. Black and the man with him and have a come-to-Jesus meeting with them. Much as I wanted to stay as far away from the man as I could, it felt like the coward's way out.

"Not in this lifetime, baby." Bear didn't even look back as he readied himself, dressing in black jeans, a black T-shirt, and his MC vest.

"Bear, please." I approached him from behind and laid a hand lightly on his back. "This is something I need to do. I have to face this."

"No." He growled, low in his chest, but the menace in it was clear. "No fuckin' way." He didn't even turn around.

I changed tactics. "You know, we had the most fantastic sex in the world, and I don't know your real name."

That made him stiffen. His shoulders rose and

fell once as he took in a deep breath before turning around. "It's Gailyn. Gailyn Hoover."

I smiled up at him. "My last name's Garrison."

"Yeah. Crush found it when he went digging. Different last name than your father." They *had* gone digging. I'd never mentioned my father's name.

"I'm not his biological daughter. I was two when he and my mother married."

"You call him your father. Not stepfather. Yet he didn't give you his name?"

I shrugged. "My family is complicated. He insisted I call him Father. Not by his first name or indicate in any way I was a stepdaughter."

"Then why not give you his name? Or adopt you?"

"That's something you'd have to ask him. Honestly, I think it kept a distance between us. He was good to me growing up, but the second my mother died, everything changed."

"What happened to your mother?" He'd stopped getting ready to leave and moved closer to me, reaching out to brush a stray curl out of my eyes.

"Honestly? I don't know. I came home from boarding school for summer break, and my father told me she'd died. I had questions but he just said it wasn't important. All that mattered was that she'd passed away, and I needed to accept it and move on."

Bear's eyes widened. "Accept it and move on?"

"Yeah. I was thirteen and more than a little terrified of him. Always had been. So I didn't question him any further. My mother and I were never really close or anything. I was probably closer to the nannies and teachers at my school than I was her. But it still hurt."

"Come here, baby." He pulled me into his arms.

"I'm sure it hurt." He rested his chin on my head, his arms wrapped solidly around me.

I took a breath. "I never want my children to feel the way I felt, Bear. I want them to know they're loved by both their parents."

"That's something you never have to worry about. I never thought I'd have kids, but when you're ready we'll have as many as you want. And I will make sure with every breath I take they know they're loved."

I snuggled against his chest for several seconds before looking up at him. "I need to do this, Bear. My father might not be with them, but I'm betting they know more about my life than I do. If they're blackmailing my father, then I know they do."

"Let me take care of this, then we'll confront your father together."

"Bear..."

"No, Liv. This guy is dangerous." He gripped my shoulders and leaned down to make his point. "My brothers and me would protect you with our lives, but I'd rather not take the chance and put you at risk in the first place. I won't lose you just when I found you."

"You won't lose me. I'll do exactly what you say without question, but I want to be there. I want them to know they don't intimidate me. Not anymore."

"They don't matter, Liv. Their opinions don't mean shit. You're not doin' their biddin' no more. I'll make that clear. Whatever they decide to do with that information doesn't matter."

"No. It's my father who'll pay. I'm good with that. But Mr. Black is the man who sent me here. I think he saw it as a one-way trip, but that the ends justified the means."

"He sent you here... to die? And you went?"

I shrugged. "Everything in my life has always been about what my dad wanted. Most of the friends I made in school had families that were the same way. I guess I knew it wasn't right, but I went along with it because he's all I have left."

"No, baby. Not anymore. You've got me. Once you get settled in, you'll have everyone here too. Apple already thinks the world of you, and you haven't known her much longer than me."

I smiled. "Apple is a wonderful person. I need to apologize to her for using what she gave me in trust against the club."

"You didn't. You did what you were supposed to do. You came to us, and we'll keep you safe."

Bear's assurance wrapped around me like a blanket, his embrace solid and unyielding. The club behind him was a fortress, a brotherhood that didn't just offer protection -- they provided a sense of belonging that I had never known in my life of privilege and isolation. They'd all given me a small taste of that inclusiveness and I wanted more. I wanted it all.

"I know you mean well, Bear," I whispered, pressing my face against the warm leather of his cut. "But this isn't just about safety. It's about facing my past, ripping out its roots so it doesn't poison my future."

Bear pulled back slightly, his eyes scanning mine with a mix of frustration and admiration. "You're one tough little pixie, aren't you?" He brushed a gentle thumb over my bottom lip before dipping his head to kiss me in a soft, lingering kiss. Then, with a sigh, he pressed his forehead to mine. "You have to do exactly what I tell you, or I'll have a prospect cart your ass away and keep you at a distance until this is finished."

I smiled up at him. "Thank you."

We walked to the common room together to meet with the others. Rocket wasn't happy with me going, but, surprisingly, Lemon was on my side.

"Women are tougher than you think. If she needs to face her fears, we can keep her safe while she does it."

"Lemon..." Rocket growled at his woman. For the first time, I could tell the difference in Rocket and Lemon when they were president and vice president versus when they were a couple. The two situations weren't mutually exclusive.

"No, Rocket," she pressed. "I'll keep an eye on her. She'll be safe." The two shared a look. I finally realized what they were saying with their looks alone.

"I'm not going to betray the club," I said softly. "I told Bear everything I know and what I was supposed to do." I looked up at Bear helplessly. "I didn't realize this was a concern for the club, though I should have. I'll stay. I don't want to put anyone in danger or put eyes on me that should be on Mr. Black."

Rocket nodded at Bear, a silent communication much like he and Lemon shared evident in the two men. "All right," Rocket said. "You can go. We'll take a couple extra guys so everyone has a watch on everyone else." His gaze settled on me. "I know Bear's claimed you, but I need to know you understand. He'll fight me. Might even win a battle between us if it's over you, but you know there will be harsh consequences if you betray us."

"I have no intention of doing anything to put the club at risk, but I understand why you have to be sure. I've been here a very short time. The only thing you know is that I was sent to infiltrate your home. Anyone would be suspicious."

"Good." Lemon snaked her arm around mine like we were best friends. I knew she was corralling me. She'd taken on the job of watching over me and keeping me out of mischief. "Let's get this over with, so we can come back to an epic orgy."

Falcon, one of the members I'd met briefly, choked on the beer he was finishing, snorting the brew out his nose as he laughed and coughed at the same time. "The fuck?" He got out the words between coughs as he wiped his face with the back of his arm until someone handed him a paper towel. "Where the fuck does she come up with this shit?"

Rocket grinned widely. "My woman's mind is very... fertile."

Lemon gave her man a brilliant smile. "And you love it. Makes for all kinds of interesting situations."

"Can't deny that." Rocket kissed the top of her head as he passed by. "Let's ride."

Chapter Nine

Bear

We sat outside the shitty little run-down motel where Leon Black and Boon were camped out. "Fuckin' place shoulda been condemned years ago." I grumbled as I studied the place with binoculars.

"Pretty sure it was." Like me, Ringo was studying the place. "Is it even still open?"

"Nope." Crush was back at the clubhouse but keeping tabs on us. "They chose this spot because they think the road across the street is the entrance to our lair. Strong evidence we're being successful in covering our tracks when we go to and from the city."

"You sure someone can't track your signal straight to us, Crush?"

"Nah, Fang," Crush drawled. "I thought I'd lead them straight to our door for shits and giggles."

Falcon snorted. "Stay in your lane, bro."

Fang grumbled. "Right. Sorry, Crush." The younger man had come to us about a year ago after an exfil had gone wrong. He'd been left for dead but had managed to literally crawl his way out. Falcon had found him and brought him to us. Fang was a good guy, but trying way too hard to fit in.

"Give your sister mine and Byte's *Fortnite* handles, and I'll call it even." I could hear the amusement in Crush's voice, but I had to wonder exactly how much he was teasing. Ariana was the only family Fang had. He'd been trying to get her to move to the compound but she'd yet to agree.

"You get her to move to the compound and I will."

"Give me a couple weeks." It was the standard answer to that same demand.

Crush had never spoken to Ariana as far as I knew. Neither had Byte. Both men had pretty much fallen in love with her picture and bickered constantly in front of Fang about which brother would marry Ariana, just to get a rise out of him. It never worked. Though, if the girl did move to the compound, I had to wonder if things would stay so congenial.

"I'll do it in one," Byte said in the background of the radio.

"In your dreams," was Crush's response. As always.

"I may have to kill one or both of them," Fang muttered. "They're not serious, are they?" He looked at Falcon for reassurance.

"About wanting your sister in the safety of the compound? Absolutely."

"The fuckers both want her!" Fang looked ready to do murder, but Falcon just chuckled.

"They're yankin' your chain, bro."

"Uh-huh," Lemon said with a grin. "We takin' bets?" She blew a bubble, then sucked it back in with a *pop*.

"Can we please get back to business?" Ringo sounded annoyed, but I saw the twitch to his lips.

"They're two blocks away," Crush interrupted. He was all business now. "Dark blue Chevy pickup. They usually park half a block away and walk around back."

"I've got them," I said, adjusting my binoculars to bring the truck in question into focus. "Yep. I recognize both men. I assume there's an entrance at the back of the building?"

"Homemade entrance," Crush confirmed. "Someone knocked a hole in the back wall. They've reinforced it a bit, but it's their way in, thinking no one will see them."

"Boon's smarter'n that," I muttered. "What's he playin' at?"

"Bear?" Rocket put a hand on my shoulder. "What're you thinkin'?"

I lowered the field glasses and met my president's gaze. "That Boon's either lost his mind or he's trying to get Black caught."

"This fuckin' guy wanted to be director of the CIA," Lemon scoffed. "Why is he not smarter'n that?"

I snorted. "If I had to guess, I'd say he was following Boon's lead."

"And Boon is about to get revenge for going to prison," Lemon guessed, probably correctly.

I shrugged, glancing at Rocket. "Can't think of anything else off the top of my head."

"Bear?" Ringo still had his field glasses to his face, gazing intently at the shitty motel. "What's that on the corner of the building next to the room Crush pegged them in?"

I took a look. "I don't see anything."

"Parallel to the bottom right corner of the window, at the edge of the stone wall."

I surveyed the area carefully. Then I saw it. "Our old outfit's insignia."

"You guys were PsyOps?" Falcon raised his eyebrows in surprise.

I shrugged. "Started in the Army together. It's how the CIA found us."

"You think he's playing a mind game?" That was the first time Olivia had spoken since we started out. She was obedient and did her best to stay out of everyone's way. Lemon was at her side constantly, and Liv didn't protest. Even now, she spoke softly.

I shrugged. "Could be, but, honestly, Boon

wasn't that kind of guy. Sure, he was really good at his job, but he's more the bust 'em in the nuts kinda guy."

"Huh." Lemon grunted. "Sounds like my kinda guy."

Rocket pointed a threatening finger at her. "Watch it, sour puss."

Lemon just grinned, flipping him off.

"Crush? Anyone hangin' back? They got a sleeper waitin' for us?"

"Negative," the other man said. "Just the two of them. I've hacked the Chevy's computer, which led to a whole lotta shit with Black's phone. I'd say your guy Boon is definitely setting him up for something."

"Gettin' us to do the dirty work," Ringo muttered. "Don't like it, but I can't see anything suspicious from this angle."

"Nothin' inside but the two of them now," Crush offered. "I was going to give the go ahead, Rocket."

"I don't want the women down there," Rocket said. "We'll nab the fuckers and take 'em to that little huntin' cabin on the edge of our territory. It's still in the middle of nowhere, and we can do what we need to."

"Also, plenty 'a gators out there." Scrub was always looking for ease of clean up. He shrugged. "Be easier to get rid of, but I can clean up wherever you decide to take care of business."

Surprisingly, Lemon didn't argue. "That's our cue to get back in the truck." Lemon urged Olivia away but she balked, looking up at me.

"Lemon's right," I said. "Go with her. You'll still get your answers, but you'll do it where I can make sure you're safe."

She nodded at me. "OK." I turned to go. "Bear?" I turned back to face her. She was wringing her hands, tears glistening in her eyes. "Please be careful. Don't..." She closed her eyes and two tears flowed down her cheeks. "Don't get hurt. No matter what."

I tilted my head at her, taking a step closer so we were nearly touching. "What's wrong, honey? You're gonna get your answers. I swear it."

She shook her head, more tears falling. "No, Bear." She reached out and grasped my vest in one small fist. "I don't... I don't think I care much anymore. Just don't get hurt. Nothing else matters."

"Liv, honey? What are you saying?" She trembled where I touched her, her slim body shaking even though it was hot and humid in the evening.

She stood there for several seconds, her gaze firmly locked with mine. Then she threw herself into my arms, wrapping herself around me. "I don't care! I don't care if I know anything! Can we just go? What if he's ready for you and tries to kill you, Bear?" Her words were barely above a whisper, but I heard her clearly.

"I expect he probably will, honey. But I've got my brothers. We've got each other's backs. It's why I'd prefer you stay away until we've got control of the situation. Fighting a skilled enemy is one thing. Fighting a skilled enemy while protecting something very precious to you is something else entirely. I have no desire to die right when I've found you, so you're staying with Lemon. Falcon and Leather will keep you safe. Then we'll all do this together."

"You promise me? You'll be OK?"

I grinned at her. "Yeah, baby. I'll be fine." I squeezed her shoulders before turning back to Rocket and the rest of my brothers. Not for the first time I was struck at how much the club had started coming together as a family. Though I'd always known I could count on the men here to have my back if I needed them, I could never remember ever feeling more sure of them as my family than I had these last few months since Lemon came to Rocket.

Finally, Liv turned away and followed Lemon to the cage to wait on us. If all went well, it would only take a few minutes to secure both men and take them back to our territory to be questioned.

We made our way to the abandoned motel. The hole in the wall was hidden, but obvious when one knew it was there. I was careful as I entered, paying close attention to everything around me. If Boon was going to betray me, it would be the second I was fully inside.

Ringo entered behind me. We had knives instead of guns since we were so close to the city. The last thing we wanted was to bring the police straight to us. Rocket and Scrub followed.

I could hear the two men talking. Leon Black and Boon. Arguing.

I glanced back at Rocket who nodded. Ringo took the lead, kicking in the door and snagging the first man he came to. Which happened to be Black. Boon raised his hands wide and above his head. He didn't look surprised.

"'Bout fuckin' time," Boon muttered as Rocket tied his hands.

"You can tell us all about it in a bit." Ringo said as he finished binding, gagging, and blindfolding Black. Where Black struggled, Boon stood passively as he was packaged the same as Black.

As I put a black bag over Boon's head, he met my gaze with a steady one of his own. There was no pleading or smirking. No expression on his face at all. I knew Boon fairly well. Or had. It was years ago. He'd changed. I knew I certainly had. Trust didn't come easily to me, and there was every possibility this was a setup. Though, for the life of me, I couldn't figure out how.

Then I shoved the bag over his head, and Ringo took him to the trailer we were pulling with the truck.

I climbed into the back seat with Olivia. She gave me a relieved look when I slid in beside her. I shut the door and reached for her hand. She took it and squeezed hard.

"Told you I'd be all right."

She nodded and gave me a watery smile. "Yeah. You did."

We made the ride in silence. Rocket and Lemon were in the front with Rocket driving, and everyone else was in the trailer with our prisoners. It took thirty minutes before we left the road, then another forty-five to reach the shed on the edge of the property. Part of it was distance, but the terrain wasn't exactly made for speed.

Rocket stopped the truck as we neared the cabin. "Close enough." He turned to look at me. "You ready?"

"Oh yeah. Been ready for this for a while."

"Let's get to it then."

* * *

Olivia

My heart was pounding. I had to concentrate on taking deep breaths so I didn't pass out. I'd been terrified of Mr. Black from the moment I'd met him. My father had made it clear he couldn't -- or wouldn't -- protect me from Mr. Black. And the man had taken an interest in me from the moment he'd met me. I was about to find out why, and I didn't have a very good feeling about how the encounter would go.

I waited with Lemon until Bear let us know he was ready for me. Then I followed Lemon in and wasn't too ashamed to admit I let her stand between me and Mr. Black. My own personal monster. I knew it showed weakness, but I'd basically been conditioned to panic when I saw Mr. Black. Yeah, he'd hit me before, but it was more the thinly veiled threats of something worse than a smack or two if I didn't do exactly what he told me.

Ringo stepped away and both Black and the other man were tied with their wrists bound above their heads. He'd removed the bags and gags they'd had on when the men had brought them back to the truck. The one Bear had called Boon didn't say anything or struggle, while Black was furious.

"I was only going to throw you in prison before this, Bear. Now I'm going to fucking bury you!"

"Why are you here, Leon?" Bear calmly asked. "Why come after me after all these years?"

"You cost me everything, Bear. You honestly think I wouldn't come for revenge?"

"And you?" I glanced at Boon. Of the two men, he was easily the most dangerous and intelligent. Black was a pimple on a gnat's ass compared to Boon. "You here for revenge, too?"

"Yep. Been wantin' revenge since I went to prison after Tripoli."

There was something about the way Boon smirked. He glanced at Black when he did. I got the feeling there was more than he was letting on.

"Well, the only one getting revenge is me," I said, stepping back and crossing my arms over my chest. "But before we get to my revenge, I have some questions."

Boon grinned. "I'll be happy to answer any questions you have."

Black snorted. "Fuck you."

Bear held out his hand in my direction. I took it as my cue to come forward. There was no way to suppress the shiver as Black's gaze met mine. He scowled and tried to lunge in my direction, but his bonds held. Ringo punched him in the abdomen with one swift, hard jab.

"There'll be none of that, asshole."

Black grunted but made no other sound. He did glare back up at Ringo.

"Why me?" I said in a soft voice. I wasn't the strong, independent woman I'd tried to be while working for my father. I was a scared girl just trying to understand how and why her life had gone to hell. "Why did you send me here?"

Black laughed. It sounded pained but definitely amused. "You're exactly the type of woman Bear goes for. I knew if I threw a woman in his path who'd been smacked around or was in immediate danger, he'd rush in like the fucking knight in shining fucking armor." He gave Bear a superior smirk. "After all these years, I still have you pegged, you bastard."

"Can't deny that," Bear said with a shrug. "Took to her from the second she jumped into my arms, and I won't deny it."

"Well, I guess you did your job after all," Mr. Black sneered at me. "Did you fuck him? I told you you'd get a lot of information from him if you fucked him."

I sucked in a breath. I couldn't help it. "That's not what happened, Bear."

He lifted the corner of his lips in a half smile. "I know."

Mr. Black chuckled. "So you did follow instructions."

"What exactly are you looking for, Leon?" Bear looked annoyed. Like he was done with this and wanted to move on. Did he believe Black? Was he regretting taking responsibility for me? Did he regret what we'd done together earlier? That thought gutted me. Sex with Bear had been the best thing to ever happen to me. I knew, realistically, we couldn't have any kind of meaningful long-term relationship. Bear was way the hell outta my league and I wasn't too proud to admit it.

"I wanted to ruin your life the way you ruined mine."

"How'd you find us?" Bear continued as if Black's answer meant nothing. I could tell by the look in his eyes he was filing everything away for later.

"Stumbled across you in Palm Springs. Just happened to see your face in the crowd and followed you. That's when I realized I could finally get you back." He grinned. "Did you fall for her or was she merely a good fuck to you?"

Bear crossed his arms over his chest, planting his legs a shoulder-length apart. "Oh, yeah. I fell for her. Made her my woman."

Mr. Black threw back his head and laughed. "Of course you did. But I really didn't think you could be led around by your dick that quickly. She hasn't had her claws in you a full day. She must have some magical pussy."

Bear popped him in the nose. Blood spurted on both sides of Black's face, and the man screamed.

"Jesus, Leon," Boon snarled. "You're makin' me look bad."

Bear turned his attention to Boon then. "So? Here

I am. What revenge do you want on me?"

"Never said I was gettin' revenge on you, Bear. Only that I was gettin' revenge." Boon jerked his head in Black's direction. "He's the reason I was in prison. Not you. You offered me a way out, and I was a fool and didn't take it. That's on me."

Bear tilted his head at Boon. "How exactly you gettin' revenge on him?"

"Figured you guys'd take care of him, given all the shit he did to get here." Boon turned his gaze to me then. "I'm sorry about this, Olivia. I was going to get you out of there until I saw Bear and realized we'd run into the very person Leon wanted to destroy. I knew you'd be safe with Bear. Even if he suspected you to be a spy, he'd have protected you until he got all the facts. Letting this go down the way it did was the only way to get you away from Leon and your father."

"What's Leon got on her old man?" Bear asked.

"What hasn't he got? Martin Calhoun is into every dirty deal in the northern hemisphere. He's ripped off so many countries it's a wonder he's still alive. Not to mention the grooming and trafficking he's done with underage girls."

Boon nodded at me. "This was his first run at Olivia. Assuming she'd done what Leon wanted, she'd have been out and home in a couple of weeks at most. Calhoun was going to start using her to appease his various clients. He hadn't done so before now because he needed her educated. She needed to be able to converse about any topic to better suit his needs. Leon threatened to expose him. To bring charges of human trafficking and running a pedophile ring. Last thing he wanted was to end up in prison. Rich or not, we all know how things go for pedophiles in prison."

"So he sold out his daughter." Bear didn't word

it as a question.

"That man would sell out his own mother if it suited him. Considering Olivia is his stepdaughter, he never batted an eye."

I felt like I was going to shatter. I hadn't loved my father. Not really. It was more the idea of having a father that appealed to me. But hearing this man laying it out so bluntly cut me to the bone.

"Liv, look at me." Bear's voice was pure command. I hesitated, but only because I wasn't sure I could stand it if I saw anger in his face. Trust didn't come easy, and I'd already lied to him. Hell of a way to start out a relationship. I was afraid he'd remember that and question himself.

"You know she's lying, Bear. Anything she told you when you fucked her was bedroom play." Black's voice was nasal from when Bear had broken his nose, but he still sounded strong and confident. "She was pumping you for information she intended to pass on to me."

Bear turned and made eye contact with Lemon. "Is this guy for real?"

Lemon's eyes widened. "You're asking me? He's your buddy."

"He's a fuckin' motherfucker," Bear spat. "He has absolutely no idea what happened or was said between me and Liv."

"Oh, hell no. He's tryin' to sow seeds of doubt." Lemon moved closer to Black. "I'm not really sure what he's trying to accomplish, though. Liv's one of us." She gave the man a wicked sneer. "We don't turn our backs on family."

"She's just a little whore," Black said with a chuckle. "She's nothing to you."

"She's everything to me, Leon," Bear said softly.

"So yeah. I guess you know me just as well today as you did when I was under your command."

"Fuck you, Bear. Just pull the fuckin' trigger and get it over with."

"I'm good with that." Lemon pulled out a gun and fired at Mr. Black... but there wasn't a report. Instead, two wires shot from the gun to Black's chest, and his body stiffened and his face contorted in pain. He opened his mouth as if to scream, but nothing came out.

"Lemon," Rocket sighed. "How many times have I told you not to carry a taser? You're loud enough with that fucking pink bike you commandeered from Falcon. Carrying weapons makes you stick out even more."

Lemon gave Rocket a blank, innocent look. "Is that really even possible?"

Rocket barked out a laugh. So did Boon and I. "Good point, baby." Rocket chuckled. Then he turned to Boon. "So, what about you?"

"I came here originally to kill Leon. But when I got there, he'd already started the move with Olivia. It was when I realized how much a pawn she was, and knew I couldn't leave her to fend for herself. So I sat back and watched until yesterday evening. I knew you were with Grim Road, Bear. I remembered what you'd told me. Working with Leon for the last few weeks also gave me time to study you guys and dig deeper into your reputation around the area." He shrugged. "No one had a bad thing to say about Grim Road. Not only that, but then you turned out to be the first club member she was able to get close to in the right setting. Like I said before. Once I knew you were the man who had her, I knew she'd be safer with you than she would be with her father."

"Olivia?" Bear pulled me into his arms. "You got any other questions for either of them?"

I shook my head, burying my face in Bear's chest. "I just want to go home. Maybe this wasn't such a good idea."

"What? Confronting Leon here?"

"Yes." The word was more of a sob. "I just want to go home with you and forget about all this."

"Thank fuck," Bear said, squeezing me to him tighter. "For a second there, I thought you meant you didn't think being with me was a good idea."

That shocked me, so I pulled back to cup his bearded face in my hands. "Bear, being with you is the best idea I've ever had."

"Someone fucking shoot me," Black snapped, disgust clear in his voice. "Pathetic!"

"You heard the man," Lemon said. "Shoot him. Bear, take Liv to the truck. We'll be there in a minute."

"Now, wait just a Goddamned minute!" There was a sharp gunshot, then silence. Bear kept my face against his chest with one big, strong hand on the back of my head.

"What about Boon?" Ringo looked to Rocket for instructions.

"Cut him loose." Rocket addressed Boon, "You want to stay with us? Prospect?"

Boon rubbed his wrist when Ringo cut him down. "I think maybe I would, Rocket."

"What about your family?" Bear turned us but didn't let me go or move my head to look at Boon. "The reason you didn't come before was because you didn't want to uproot them."

"My wife divorced me when I was in prison. My kids are grown and don't want anything to do with me." He shrugged. "I thought I'd maybe get a fresh start."

"Crush will have to look into your background, but if Bear vouches for you, we'll take you in."

"Bear vouches for him," Bear said. "Now, I'm takin' my woman out of here. Boon, good to see you. Hate all the shit you went through, but I'm glad you found your way here."

"Thanks Bear. I owe you."

"Anytime, brother. We're family here. Welcome aboard."

Chapter Ten

Bear

The ride back to the clubhouse took some time. Not only was the terrain less than ideal, but Crush wanted us to take the scenic route and do a few double backs to make sure no one was following us. Or that we didn't have some kind of tracking device on us. It wasn't exactly standard after what we'd done, but he and Byte wanted to be careful since we had no idea where the tech on Liv's phone came from.

A couple hours -- and a different vehicle -- later we rolled through the compound gates. Yeah. The paranoia from Crush was just too great to risk bringing the truck back, so we sold it to a guy named Red at Red's Garage in Palm Beach. The guy was road captain for Salvation's Bane. After giving him the rundown, he swapped us a truck and set about making ours disappear. Not my business how. That was Ringo's department. All I was concerned with was taking care of my girl.

Liv clung to me, sitting sideways on my lap. Her slender arms were around my neck, her face against my chest.

She was silent, the kind of silence that spoke volumes, her breathing uneven at times as we rolled onto safe ground. Every now and then, her grip on me tightened like she was reminding herself I was real, that she wasn't alone. It did something fierce to my heart, knowing how much she relied on me.

When we finally pulled in front of our little house inside the family area of our compound, the sense of relief was palpable.

There were several of the guys waiting outside for us. Bullet approached first, his sharp-eyed gaze scanning Olivia before he looked up at me. "You guys need anything?"

"I think we're good," I said, exiting the vehicle with Liv in my arms. "Maybe have a prospect bring some stuff for sandwiches and some drinks."

Apple darted from inside the house and ran straight to us. "Is she all right? What'd you do to her, Bear?" Her face looked as fierce as Lemon always did. Like she was ready to take a motherfucker down. In this case, the motherfucker in question was me.

"She's fine," I said, fighting the grin tugging at my lips. "Been a rough day for her. She's gonna need you, Apple. Once I get her settled and she's had time to rest."

"You say the word and I'm there. I'll stay with her now if she needs me."

Liv shifted then, turning to look at Apple. "Thank you, Apple. For everything."

"I didn't do anything, honey."

"You helped me get into Grim Road. I'm sorry I used it as a way to get inside to spy, but you brought me to Bear."

Apple waved off my comment. "These guys are more than capable of taking care of themselves and you clearly needed help. Maybe not like I'd first thought, but close enough."

"You didn't even know me that well, Apple. You went out on a limb to help a stranger. I'll always be grateful for that."

"Just take care of Bear there. He's got it pretty hard around here. None of the club girls want him. I damn sure don't want him." She tapped a finger on her lips as if contemplating her next words. "You know, he's not nearly good enough for you. Maybe I better look for someone else for you."

I growled at Apple, who grinned up at me with a superior smirk on her lips. Thankfully, Olivia gave a little chuckle.

"Nah. Think I'll keep him. He's already semi-housebroken. I'd hate to waste all that time and effort."

"Brat," I grumbled, but kissed her lips gently. "But you're my brat."

Apple gave a crisp nod. "Good. I'll spread the word you're taken, Bear." She grinned at Olivia. "You have my number. You need anything, call me. It's what best friends are for."

Olivia blinked down at Apple. "Best friends? I-I've never had a best friend before."

"Good. That way there's no expectations, I can protect you as much as I see fit, and Bear here can have me bust his balls when he needs it and you can't get mad 'cause you think I'm being overprotective. 'Cause that's what best friends do." Apple shrugged. "At least, according to Lemon. I never have in the past, but I'm thinking about taking it up."

That got a chuckle out of me. "You're supposed to be the docile one."

"Yeah?" she asked, raising an eyebrow. "Never heard that before."

"I'll have Lemon work on getting you guys a bigger place in the family section. While I'm sure your digs here are fine, Liv deserves better."

"Fully aware, hellcat."

Apple smirked. "I think I like that. When I get to be an enforcer in the club, that's what my road name's gonna be."

"Heaven help us all if that happens." That came from Falcon as he passed us on the way back to the clubhouse.

Apple chucked her empty soda can at the back of

his head. It hit with deadly accuracy. "Ain't no 'if,' bitch. My sister is vice president. Imma be an enforcer."

"Rocket! Your sister-in-law's being a pain in the ass!" Falcon called to the president, never looking back at Apple, though he did duck his head and rubbed the back of it where her can had hit.

"Deal with it, fucker," Rocket called back. "I got my hands full with my vice president right now." He chuckled. "Literally. My hands are full of her ass while she's straddlin' me on the couch."

Liv jerked and peeked around me to find Rocket and a grinning Lemon on the couch just like Rocket said. She faced him, straddling his hips. And, of course, Rocket gripped her jeans-clad ass in a firm grip before letting one side go and smacking a hand down on her cheek in a hard slap. Lemon yelped but immediately giggled and wiggled over his crotch.

"OMG! Get your ass back to the clubhouse or something and get a room, you guys!" Apple rolled her eyes, but she couldn't fight the grin spreading her lips.

All this made Liv laugh too. So, yeah. I was grateful to both women. And Rocket. My whole club, really. They'd come through with flying colors for us.

I took us to my room and kicked the door shut before sitting on the bed with Olivia still in my arms. "You all right?" I murmured into her hair, feeling every shiver that rippled through her body.

"Yeah, just..." She paused, lifting her head to look into my eyes. "It's a lot, you know? Everything that went down today."

I nodded, my hand stroking down her back. "I know, honey. But you're safe now. You're with me. We're with the club."

She gave me a tired smile and nestled back

against me. In the distance, the clubhouse was loud tonight, full of the raucous laughter and chatter of the Grim Road brothers. Each night seemed to get louder and louder. It should have been annoying, but I found it comforting. It was the noise of a big family get-together. Once Liv and I were properly settled and comfortable with each other and our place in each other's lives, I looked forward to participating with her in the common room. But right here, right now, in my arms, it felt like we were the only two people in the world. I loved it.

"Kiss me, baby," I said in a rough voice. "Want to feel your lips on mine."

Without hesitation, Olivia tilted her head up, her pale eyes locking onto mine with an intensity that caught my breath. Her lips met mine in a soft, tentative touch that quickly deepened as she threaded her fingers through the short hair at the back of my neck, pulling me closer.

As our kiss grew fierce and demanding, I could feel every barrier between us melting away. The world outside -- the noise of the clubhouse, the constant threats surrounding the Grim Road MC -- everything faded into insignificance. In that moment, there was only Liv, her warmth, her taste, and the undeniable connection that had somehow formed between us amidst chaos.

Breaking the kiss momentarily, I stared down into her lovely eyes. I was struck at how much this woman meant to me in such a short time. The longer I spent in her presence, the more I wanted her. Body and soul. I wanted the right to claim all of her.

Liv's response was immediate and full of yearning. She leaned in again, her lips meeting mine in a sweet, fierce kiss that spoke of all the turmoil of the day. Her arms slid around my neck, pulling me closer as if she needed the contact as much as I did.

The kiss deepened, and every barrier between us melted away. The taste of her was like a drug, addictive and heady, and I groaned into her mouth. My hands roamed down to grasp her hips, turning her so she straddled my lap. She gasped against my lips, a small sound of surprise and pleasure that made my heart hammer even harder.

Breathing heavily, I pulled back just enough to gaze into her eyes, those light pools reflecting a mix of desire and something fiercely possessive. She wanted me as much as I wanted her. She was mine. I was hers.

"Liv," I murmured, my voice hoarse with emotion, "I want you -- all of you. Not just tonight, but every night after. For as long as I live."

Liv bit her lip, a nervous habit I'd come to recognize and adore. She nodded slightly, her breath catching in her throat. "I-I want that too, Bear. I'm scared, but... I trust you. I've never felt like this before and I never want it to end."

My heart swelled at her words, and impulsively, I tightened my grip on her hips, bringing her closer so she sat over the hard ridge of my cock. Our clothing separated us, but I could still feel the heat of her pussy. Or I imagined I could.

Her fingers dug into my shoulders, the platinum strands of her hair cascading around us like a curtain, shielding us from the world. I felt her heartbeat racing against mine where she pressed herself against my chest as she continued to kiss me. Her breath was hot and urgent as our kiss became a fiery dance of need and desire.

"Bear..." She breathed out my name between kisses, her voice a mix of vulnerability and passion that damn near broke me. I pulled back just enough to look at her, seeing the flush spread across her cheeks, her eyes glowing with a mix of wild fear and fierce courage.

"I've got you," I whispered, my words rough with emotion. "Always."

The affirmation seemed to unleash something within her and she whipped off her shirt and fumbled with her bra. Once she was naked from the waist up, she lay back against me, rubbing her breasts over my chest like a contented kitten.

Her skin was soft, impossibly smooth against the hair-roughened texture of my tattooed skin. I molded her curves with my hands, memorizing the feel of her body as if I'd never get another chance. The dim light from the bedside lamp threw shadows across her face, highlighting the fierce determination in her eyes.

"Need you," Liv whispered, her voice husky with desire. She reached between us to tug at the button of my jeans, her fingers dancing over my belly to touch more of me. I helped her shove my jeans down my hips before lifting her off me to stand in front of me.

It didn't take long after that for Liv to strip completely. I did the same, watching her avidly, eating up the beautifully erotic sight of the fine, smooth muscles playing under her skin as she moved.

"So fuckin' sexy," I growled.

Liv's eyes widened, a shimmer of something wild flickering across her features as she watched me. She stood there, stark naked in front of me. She bit her lip, that nervous but eager gesture that drove me wild, and stepped closer. Her hands reached out, tentative at first, then with more confidence as they traced the lines of my chest, over my abs, and down farther.

"God, Bear," she whispered, a tremor in her voice as she explored my skin. "You're... incredible."

I pulled her against me, moving us onto the bed. As I lay on top of her, my larger frame dwarfed her slight figure. My hands slid around to cradle the small of her back, my cock pressing against her belly.

The heat between us was palpable, a tangible force that seemed to sizzle in the small space of the room. I felt every shiver that coursed through her body as if it were traveling through mine.

"Tell me what you want, Liv," I rasped, needing to hear her say it, needing to hear that raw desire vocalized.

With a shaky breath that was part moan, she looked up at me through her thick lashes, her eyes dark with lust. "I want you to fuck me. I want it all and I don't want you to hold back."

That was all the encouragement I needed. My hands moved to her ass, lifting her effortlessly. I followed her and latched on to one ripe nipple as she settled on top of the covers.

I couldn't hold back a groan. The sound vibrated between us, filled with raw desire. My fingers traced up her side to cup the same breast I sucked from, sending shivers through her body.

My other hand tangled in her hair and tilted her head back to expose her throat. Much as I hated leaving her breast, I needed my mouth at her neck. It was a primal desire, the need to mark her where everyone could see paramount.

Liv shuddered, arching her back and exposing her neck to my mouth. She took in a deep, shuddering breath. Her hands were bold now, roaming over my back, digging into the muscles there before descending lower to grab my ass, pulling me harder against her.

"You want my cock inside you, baby?" I murmured my question against the skin of her neck. Immediately, chill bumps erupted over her skin, and she sucked in a breath.

"Yes," she breathed out. "Need you to fuck me. Hard."

"You feel so fuckin' good," I muttered against her ear, pulling her even closer, feeling the heat radiating from her body where she was mashed tightly against my cock. "Gonna eat you alive..."

Her breath hitched again, a visible shiver racing through her as anticipation tightened the air between us. Liv's eyes, alight with unbridled desire, locked onto mine, silently pleading for what only I could give her.

Without another word, I positioned myself between her thighs. Her legs wrapped around me, drawing me in closer, her hips tilting up to meet mine as I entered her. This time, I took her bare, not wanting anything to separate us. I'd deal with the fallout later. It was a dick move, but Liv was mine now. All mine and I refused to have any kind of barrier between us. The heat from her pussy was intoxicating, and I paused for a moment just to savor the sight of her laid out beneath me, impaled on my cock, so vulnerable yet so incredibly strong.

Liv's eyes flashed with desire and a hint of something fierce, almost like a challenge. Her hands, now more confident, slid over my shoulders, feeling the contours of muscle and inked skin beneath them. She leaned into my touch, her breath hitching as I continued to tease her skin with lips and teeth, marking her neck gently yet possessively.

"Bear," she moaned softly, her voice breaking through the thick air of arousal filling the room. "Don't stop... please."

Her plea was all the permission my primal side needed. I started moving with a hard, driving rhythm.

"Greedy little pussy suckin' me inside," I growled. "Gonna fuck you till you come, then gonna put my cum inside that same greedy little pussy."

"Oh God! Bear!" Liv's eyes were shut tightly as she cried out, arching her neck backward again. I latched on to her neck, continuing to fuck her hard and fast.

"Come for me, baby," I growled at her ear. "Come on my fuckin' cock and milk my cum from me."

She did. With a ragged scream, Liv exploded around me. Her pussy spasmed around me, squeezing until there was no holding back.

With a brutal yell of my own, I emptied myself deep inside her, growling in satisfaction as I did.

Her body shuddered beneath me from the waves of pleasure rolling through her. I collapsed fully on top of her as both of us gasped for breath. The room was thick with the scent of sex and sweat, a testament to the raw, unbridled passion we had just unleashed.

Liv's fingers danced lightly across my back, tracing the scars and tattoos that marked my skin. Her touch was gentle, almost reverent, as if she could heal all the old wounds that lingered beneath the surface.

"You okay?" I murmured, lifting myself up to look into her eyes. They were still filled with heat, but there was a softness there too -- a vulnerability. Like she'd shown me her soft underbelly and was afraid I'd slash her to ribbons.

"Yes."

"You know I'll never hurt you, right? You're mine and I'm yours."

"Do you promise? I mean, I know some clubs

don't think fidelity is a thing, but I can't... I can't share you." She genuinely distressed. I had to smile.

"Honey, no way in hell you're sharing me. Just like there's no way in hell I'd share you. It's you and me." I kissed her lips gently, coaxing her to kiss me back.

I brushed a strand of platinum hair from her face, watching her in the aftermath of our passion. "That what you needed, baby?" I asked, my voice rough with residual desire.

Liv's eyes fluttered open, and she smiled -- a genuine, soul-deep smile that did something to my heart, knowing I was the one to put that look on her lovely face.

"Yeah, exactly what I needed," she whispered, her voice husky from her screams of pleasure. Her fingers traced a pattern on my chest, light and ticklish, making me grin like a fool under her touch.

I rolled off her, pulling her close into my side, feeling the need to hold her tight against me. The bed creaked under our combined weight, a reminder of the reality of everything between us. Liv snuggled closer, resting her head on my chest. The sound of her steady breathing mixed with the distant hum of life outside our room.

The club party was in full swing. Music blared, though muffled by the walls and distance. It was both annoying and filled me with joy.

"What is it?" She leaned up on one elbow, touching the corners of my lips. "You're smiling."

"That a crime?" I tried to give her a mock growl, but spoiled it by not being able to wipe the grin off my face.

"Not at all." Her smile was contented, and I hoped I could keep that look on her face. "Just wondering what you're thinking."

"That my woman and my club are all coming together. The two most important things in my life and I have them right here. Safe. With me."

Liv's eyes softened, reflecting the dim light that filtered through the curtains, giving her an ethereal glow. "That means everything to me, Bear. *You* mean everything."

I pulled her closer, burying my face in her hair, inhaling the scent of her shampoo mixed with the smell of sex. "You're safe here, Liv. With me, with the club. We're your family now."

Her voice was tender, barely above a whisper. "I never had much of a family, Bear. But being here with you, with all of them... it feels right. Even no longer than I've been here."

The statement hit me harder than any punch I'd ever taken. This fierce, beautiful woman had found her place in the chaos of our world, and it was by my side. I felt a surge of protectiveness, mixed with a profound gratitude.

"Do you know what's going to happen to my father?"

"No. But given what he's done, I'm sure Rocket and Lemon won't let him get off scot-free. That will take them some time to work out, though." Then a thought struck me. "That bother you?"

"What? No! Of course not! He's the one who let me get put in this situation to begin with. Though, given how things turned out -- with you and the club and the feeling that I finally have a real home -- maybe I owe him a debt of gratitude."

"Just because you ended up better than you were to begin with doesn't negate what he did. You don't owe him anything, honey."

"He might come after me, you know. He was never very good at being told no."

"We'll look out for each other," I promised, knowing full well my brothers and sisters could take anything thrown our way. Including a narcissistic megalomaniac. Grim Road MC wasn't just a club -- it was a sanctuary, a fortress against the outside world that would just love to destroy us.

The sounds of raucous laughter and the thump of heavy bass filtered through the walls, but it all faded away as I held her. The world outside could fall into chaos, but in this moment, with Liv in my arms, everything was perfect.

"You think we can keep this peace?" she asked quietly, a hint of worry threading her voice.

I tightened my grip around her, protective instincts flaring up. "As long as I'm breathing, nothing touches this peace. Nothing touches us."

She nestled farther into me, her body relaxing as if my words had fortified her own strength. We lay there for a while, a lazy lethargy stealing over me.

"Bear?"

"Yeah, baby."

"Is it too soon to tell you I love you?"

I couldn't help the smile tugging my lips and didn't try to fight it. "If it is, then I'm guilty. Because I love you, too. Ain't ashamed to admit it neither."

"Good. 'Cause I do. Love you, that is."

And that's how I drifted off, Liv's warm body securely in my arms, her words of love in my ears.

Ringo (Grim Road MC 6)
A Bones MC Romance
Marteeka Karland

Calista – When my stepfather decides the best way to get himself out of trouble is to trade me to the man who owns his gambling debts, I know it's time to get the hell outta Dodge. Before she died, my mother told me my real dad was a hero, but what he'd done in the military was so secret, he had to disappear. Just before she died, she told me the words *Dominic* and *Grim Road* -- my father's name and the group he belonged to. I can't think of anyone else I can go to for help. But once I find Grim Road's compound, I realize there are far more dangerous things waiting for me there -- like a man who could steal my heart.

Ringo: When a little spitfire walks up to the gates of Grim Road demanding to see our sergeant at arms, Dominic, I know I'm in trouble. She looks vaguely familiar, but I can't quite place her. When she refuses to leave, the prospect at the gate gives her a good, hard shove. The expression on her face of shock and fear triggers a memory. A little girl -- this girl -- falling backwards off the front porch steps into the flower bed. Calista. Dom's daughter. Only she's not a little girl anymore. She's the most stunning woman I've ever laid eyes on, and I'm gonna make her mine. I just need to figure out how to keep her father from killing me.

Chapter One

Calista

Nothing in my life could have prepared me for the last three days. I needed to get scarce. Now. Which was hard to do when my stepdad's goons kept a close eye on me.

"Back in your room, Miss Calista."

"I need to go out."

"I'm sorry, Miss Calista. We have strict orders that you are not to leave the hotel room." My bodyguard, Sam, wasn't unkind or short with me, just matter of fact. I was a job to him. Nothing more. Nothing less.

"I know what he said, Sam, but I've got a... situation and I need to go out. Just across the street to the pharmacy. That's it. I promise I'll be right back."

He narrowed his gaze at me. "The pharmacy?"

"Um, yeah." I ducked my head, wringing my hands. I was trying to look nervous and embarrassed. I'm sure I pulled off the first. The second? Well, if terrified could pass for embarrassed, maybe. "You know. Feminine products."

Sam swore under his breath, giving me a furious look as he took out his phone. That was unexpected. He was always so remote and aloof. If this didn't work, I'd be dead. If Sam didn't let me leave, if he sent someone after my tampons, I'd have to show proof. Because, you know, my stepfather had promised to sell me to some guy for a night to do whatever he wanted to me.

It sounded like it was to pay off a loan. I kind of lost the thread of the conversation after that, but the bottom line was, if they had to reschedule this little "exchange," that guy was probably going to want to know why. Which meant he would likely want proof I was on my stupid period. Given the fact my stepdad didn't think I knew what was supposed to happen, he might not be suspicious enough to prevent me from leaving for a short time while he contacted the guy. That's what I was hoping for. If I couldn't make it away, though...

Sam spoke softly, telling whoever was on the other end the situation in as few words as humanly possible. His irritation was very clear. When he put his phone away, he jerked his head in the direction of the elevator. The hotel was posh, and I was certain he could get someone to bring me what I needed. I'd chosen my ailment carefully, knowing neither my guards nor my stepfather would want to explain to anyone what I needed. Since the first thing Sam had done when he'd put me in the car to come here was take my phone, I was sure neither of them would want me to call down for it myself.

"Thanks, Sam." I hurried out the door and down the hall before he changed his mind, or my stepfather did and called Sam back. "I'll only be a minute," I called over my shoulder as I stabbed the button for the elevator. Thankfully, it opened in only a few seconds.

My heart tripped, hammering in my chest. If this didn't work, I was so screwed it wasn't even funny. Probably was anyway. My plan went past risky to completely insane, but the last thing I was going to do was to willingly go to my doom. If I got caught, at least I tried.

When I exited the hotel, I paused at the crosswalk, trying to act normal and not look like I was in a hurry. I crossed the street with the flow of the few people around me, and into the pharmacy. Once inside, I hurried through the store to the back. As luck would have it, I managed to get to the back door without being spotted. I also snagged a flashlight I spotted hanging on the wall next to the fire extinguisher which I knew would prove invaluable later. I'd chosen this time of day because it was thirty minutes after shift change at this store and the likelihood of someone being in the staff area was slim. I'd been lucky we'd been next to this particular store since it was one I knew. I was taking a chance that I'd run into someone I knew, but I had no other options.

Once out the back, I hurriedly twisted my hair into a tight bun and secured it with a hair tie. Then I stripped off the light gray slacks and matching jacket, leaving myself in a black tank and black leggings. It took every ounce of willpower I had to not look over my shoulder as I moved out onto the sidewalk. If I had any hope at all of getting away unnoticed, I needed to go now while there were still people around and the lighting was dim. It was almost twilight in the city. The streetlights hadn't all come on yet and it was hard to see at a distance.

I walked at a brisk pace for several blocks, taking as many turns as I could and still moving steadily away from the hotel. No one called out to me or gave chase. As far as I could tell, no one knew I was missing. I was hoping that, given the nature of my errand, Sam would give me several additional minutes before he went looking for me.

When I finally approached the edge of the city, I gave up all pretense of trying to blend in. I took off at nearly a sprint. The longer I was out in the open, the greater the chances Sam or one of Borris's other men would spot me. I had to make it through a few more city blocks, then across the highway -- another risk since not many people crossed on foot -- and into the woods. Once I had the cover of the trees, I'd find a place to settle down for the night and hopefully make it to the compound tomorrow. I didn't want to get lost, so I had to take the chance they wouldn't come this way looking for me. Or, if they did, that they'd wait until daylight so they had a better chance of tracking me accurately.

All I had was an old compass my mother had given me with a tiny map folded inside tucked into my bra, and the flashlight I'd stolen. No food. No water. No protection from the elements. Just the compass and map, and a flashlight. And stories of a place my mother told me about, but I'd never seen. This was all kinds of crazy, but it was my choice. No one else's.

By the time I was deep in the woods and far enough away from the road as I could safely get, it was full dark. I didn't want to use the light yet as it was early enough Sam might still make a try on the chance I hadn't gone far, and Sam might still make a try if he could figure out where I'd gone into the woods. Plus, I had no idea how long the battery would last. Hopefully a while. Though I'd thought I was prepared mentally for a couple of days out in the wild on my own, I hadn't thought about how dark it would actually be. And I wasn't even thinking about the possibility of snakes.

Or alligators.

The air was thick with humidity, and every leaf seemed to whisper nefarious secrets as I pushed farther into the undergrowth. My limbs ached, my heart pounded in my ears, and fear clung to me like the dense fog that began to roll in from the nearby swamp. The noises of the night grew louder, a cacophony of insects and distant howls that did nothing to ease my nerves.

I tried to keep my breathing steady, reminding myself that panic would only make things worse. The darkness was absolute -- even the faint glow of moonlight struggled to penetrate the thick canopy above. Every rustle in the bushes sent a spike of adrenaline through my system. Was the noise from a predator stalking me? Was it Sam? More of my stepfather's goons? I wasn't sure if I was more afraid of giant snakes or my stepfather. Borris Illivitch was a cold-hearted bastard. When he found out I'd blazed... If he caught me, I'd be in a world of pain. Death would be a release.

I pressed on, trying to use what little moonlight filtered through the tree canopy to guide my steps. Which... yeah. Occasionally, I'd see a sliver of moon, but that was it. The air grew cooler as the damp night deepened, and an occasional breeze should have felt good in the Florida humidity but only seemed to grate on my nerves instead of soothing me. Despite the risks, knowing it was a bad idea to stumble around in the dark, I felt this urgent need to press on. Keep moving. Stay ahead of the thugs I knew would be after me.

I continued on for as long as I could. When I finally reached the point where exhaustion overrode the adrenaline, I leaned against a tree. Not the smartest move, but I was beyond caring at this point. My lungs burned, as did my leg muscles. I was scraped all over, my clothes even ripped in a couple places. The only thing I'd risked in standing out with regard to my appearance was the combat boots I wore. Not uncommon, but also noticeable. Thankfully my suit pants had been flared at the bottom and had hidden them. The boots were the only things allowing me to travel as far as I had.

I knew the general direction I needed to go. My

mom had also taught me landmarks in the area to look for by using a child's nursery rhyme. All of which she told me about just days before she died. I'd long ago used virtual maps to find the landmarks she taught me. I was as prepared as I could be.

I finally stopped and took stock of my body. I had some stinging scrapes and at some point I'd twisted my ankle, but it wasn't anything I couldn't power through. As the silvery moon moved across the sky, the light filtered through the trees lessened. I could barely see my hand in front of my face, let alone anything around me. Or my compass.

I was on solid ground but had no idea what was above or around me. With the adrenaline falling off, I was trembling. Which was creating more panic. I was basically defenseless in unfamiliar territory. Yeah. It was time where the benefits of using the flashlight outweighed the risks.

I switched on the light, shining it around the area. A pair of eyes glowed back at me and I jumped back, sucking in a breath, but the little varmint ran off. At least, I hoped it was little.

"OK. OK." I was talking out loud, but really, I had to do something other than freak myself out by listening to all the noises around me. Or look for glowing predator eyes. "I got this. Mom said this place was miles and miles of swamp, trees, and forest, but if I was careful, I could make my way through all that to the place my dad lived.

It took a couple of hours, but I finally found a small, rundown shack. Looked like, at one time, it might have been a hunting cabin, or some kind of game-watch post. It wasn't much bigger than a small storage building but wasn't completely enclosed. About halfway up the walls, all around, the enclosure was open, at one time covered with a screen. Kept out insects but allowed the occupant to see out in all directions. This was a landmark on my map, and I'd basically stumbled on it.

I went inside the little shack, noting there was nothing inside except a bench fashioned all around the inside perimeter and dirt and leaves. The screens had long ago been torn or had fallen apart, leaving only ragged remnants to sway in the slight breeze.

It was ridiculous, but with a roof over my head, even with little protection from anything, I felt a little safer. Not safe, by any means, but more... secure.

I set the light beside me when I sank down onto one of the benches. Carefully, I pulled out my compass and opened it, taking care with the delicate piece of paper folded inside it. Opening it up, I confirmed what I already knew. I needed to head straight northeast. Like, this place had been put in this exact position to use as a landmark. My mother had given me three at various points around the center structure I was trying to get to. Each landmark pointed in a precise direction, so I had no doubt these spots were carefully thought out and deliberately placed as guides. If you knew the coordinates. And had a map. Which I did. A treasure map, if you will.

From my current position, I estimated it would take me about six hours to walk. It wasn't that far, per se, but walking in the woods and swamp was tricky going. The accepted estimate was to allow thirty minutes for every mile walked. I guessed I'd find out how far off that estimate was when I found the place I was looking for.

And my dad. Unfortunately, I had no idea if he knew I existed. If he did, there was every possibility he wouldn't accept me or even want me in his life. Which was fine. I just needed his protection long enough to make sure Borris Illivitch gave up looking for me.

Turned out, I made better time than I thought I would. Even in the dark. I literally stumbled into a big guy with a full beard. He scowled down at me even as his hands went to my shoulders to steady me. I expected his fingers to bite into my flesh, but he was surprisingly gentle.

"Who the fuck goes there at four-thirty in the fuckin' mornin'?"

"I..." I jumped and nearly squealed. I hadn't even heard the guy approach! He loomed over me. I couldn't see him that well, but I knew he was much larger than me. Reflexively, I shone the light on him. Huge mistake. He reached out and batted the light away from his face before grabbing the thing from me in a swift jerk that took my breath. If he was anything like the way my mom described my dad, then I had no hope of fighting him off if he chose to attack. Not for the first time, I questioned my sanity. Was this really the only option I had? I mean, besides letting my stepfather sell me to his loan shark. Taking a deep breath, I straightened, squaring my shoulders as I found my backbone. "I'm here to see Dominic."

The man stared me down for several seconds, but I refused to look away. I met his gaze boldly, leaving no mistake I intended to get what I wanted. Some of the last words my mother spoke to me were to approach these men with confidence and strength. Any show of weakness on my part and they'd simply refuse me entrance.

Finally, he snorted a laugh. "I think you're in the wrong place, little girl. Best you be moving on."

"I'm here to see Dominic and I'm not leaving until I do. Tell him Tina sent me." I held up the compass. My mother said it might be the one thing that would get me in, though she confessed she didn't know how Dominic would take the token. "Tell him I have something for him." The guy reached for the compass, but I jerked it back. "I'll give it to him myself."

"Little spitfire, eh?" There was no denying the amusement in his voice. "All right then. Wait here." He turned and left me, disappearing back into the woods.

I was so fucking tired. If this guy was right and it was four-thirty in the morning, I'd been hiking through the woods and swamp for the better part of seven hours. Not only was I exhausted, my body had gone about as far as it could.

I think I dozed off where I was standing, because the next thing I knew the guy was back with a scowl on his face. "Ringo said Dom's busy. Said to give me whatever you had and he'd give it to Dom at a decent fuckin' hour."

I closed my eyes, inhaling for patience. "Look. I've literally been hiking in unfamiliar territory the entre *fucking* night. I'm tired. I'm hungry. I'm thirsty. And more than a little cranky. Either get Dominic for me or let me in and I'll find him myself."

I took a step forward, intending to march past the man. I had no idea where to go from there because I couldn't see any sign of structures or even other people. He snagged my arm in a punishing grip, halting my progress.

"Where the fuck you think you're goin', huh?"

"I told you, dumbass. I'm here to see Dom." Fatigue was making me grouchy as shit and I knew I needed to dial it down, but my mouth wasn't picking up what my brain was putting down. "Are you deaf or just fuckin' stupid?"

The second the words left my mouth, I knew I'd made a huge mistake. Anger flashed in the guy's eyes and his hand darted to my throat, squeezing my neck nearly as hard as he'd gripped my arm.

"You don't get to talk to me that way, bitch. You're in our territory and you'll do what the fuck I tell you. Now get your fuckin' ass outta here before I have to help you out."

This wasn't happening. I might not be able to take this guy in a fight, but I wasn't about to stand here and let him strangle me. I found his pinky finger with my hands. It took everything I had left to get leverage under the digit and pry it loose from my neck.

Once I managed to dig my way underneath, I pulled with all my might, bending his finger back. Just as I'd read it would, the move loosened his grip. I thought he might use his other hand to strangle me or even hit. Instead, he shoved me backward. Hard. I stumbled and fell on my ass as he pulled a gun and cocked it, aiming it at me.

"Redwood? What the fuck are you doin'?" Another man appeared from the trees and shadow. This guy was... waaaay the fuck bigger than Redwood. Both wider and taller. If he jumped in to help his buddy, I was royally screwed.

Redwood's attention wavered and I struck. I brought my foot up sharply, hoping to catch his balls and make them sing. Even in the dark, I could manage to get close. He grunted and immediately stepped back, going down to one knee. I scrambled backward until I was sure I had my balance.

"Stop!" The second guy kicked Redwood over so the other man groaned and lay in the fetal position, clutching his crotch. Was he talking to me? "Not one more step, girl." I guess he was talking to me.

"I'm not standing here and letting that bastard strangle me to death." I bared my teeth at the guy. "I came a long fucking way to see Dominic. Either take me to him or tell him why you turned his daughter away."

I was taking a huge gamble here. I had no idea if this guy would feel any obligation to help me or not. But my mother seemed to think he would. It was why I was told to give Dominic the compass. She said it was special to him.

The newcomer stood absolutely still for several seconds. If I'd overplayed my hand, if Dominic wanted nothing to do with me, I might wish I was back with my stepfather.

"Surely you don't believe the bitch, Ringo," Redwood wheezed out. "Dom woulda said something if he had a daughter. Especially after Lemon started making sure we all took care of our families."

Ringo didn't acknowledge Redwood, only stared at me. The moonlight filtering down wasn't nearly enough for me to get a good look at the guy. Well, other than his size. Then he switched on a red light he had looped around his forehead. It wasn't much and I didn't think he could see me too clearly, but I knew enough to know it was to save his night vision. With the total pitch black in these woods, he probably needed it.

He must have seen something because he jerked back, actually taking two full steps backward. "Well, I'll be Goddamned. Calista."

Chapter Two

Ringo

I was so fucking fucked as to not even be fucking believed. I recognized this girl from pictures our sergeant at arms kept in his room at the main clubhouse. As his enforcer, he and I had grown pretty close over the years, and he'd told me some stories. He had a small table dedicated to Calista. Dom had said the girl's mother had died a few years before, but Tina had sent him pictures of Calista regularly until the woman had passed. He didn't tell me his and Tina's story and I'd never asked. This young woman before me now was definitely Calista. What Dom had failed to mention was how truly lovely the girl had become. Probably why he hadn't put a new picture of her up in a few years. Likely keeping them to himself where horny bastards like myself couldn't see them and be lusting after his daughter.

And it wasn't just her looks. Calista had spunk. She was dressed in black leggings and a black tank, but she had combat boots on her feet. She'd also ventured into our territory intentionally, which meant she'd been walking in the woods for hours.

"How do you know my name?" She gave me a wary look.

"Your father has pictures of you in his rooms in the clubhouse. Your mother sent him pictures until she died."

"What?" Her eyes widened in surprise. "She did?"

"Yeah, baby girl. Come on." I held out a hand to her and it surprised me when she took it. She must really have been tired, because the last thing she needed was to have her hands restricted in the company of men two or three times her size.

She let out a noise of distress as if suddenly realizing she'd given up a very important advantage. If you could call it that. She had fire and might be scrappy, but everyone here -- other than the women and children -- were seasoned warriors and me holding her dominant hand was a distinct disadvantage. "Ain't gonna hurt you. You're family," I tried to soothe her.

"Yeah? What about Peckerwood over there? He gonna hurt me? You know. Again?"

"It's Redwood, girlie." The prospect -- who was still trying to get to his feet -- sounded like anything but a seasoned warrior. She'd definitely gotten in a good lick. If the situation was anything else, I'd have been amused. OK, so I was still amused. This girl had fire. Maybe not as much as Lemon, but she'd get there. Did my heart proud.

"That's what I said." She blinked, all innocent and shit. "Peckerwood."

Yeah. I was fucked. Took every ounce of control I had not to outright guffaw. And my cock wanted this woman. Hard.

Redwood growled, and I tugged Calista's hand. "Come on, little hellcat. Let's go see your daddy."

I led her through the gate. The fence marking our territory boundary wasn't obvious and I'd watched her from the security station just inside the gate. She hadn't noticed the chain-link fence topped with razor wire until Redwood approached her. Not surprising, since Redwood had been prepared for her before she got to the gate and moved out to meet her. Also, even with her flashlight it was dead night and the place was camouflaged with trees and foliage. It was the time of night/very early morning when the moon sets and the sun hasn't started over the horizon. With us being in the woods, it was exceptionally dark. Even with the flashlight she brandished before Redwood had taken it from her, she'd had a hard time cutting through the dark.

The compound was dark. The only lights coming from inside houses were muted by blackout curtains. We didn't always use them, but Dom tried to keep us all aware that, you know, light carried. There were lots of trees and such to blanket us from prying eyes, but Dom was the SAA. It was his job to keep everyone safe.

We entered the main clubhouse. It was more sedate than usual. Probably because of the recent close call with Bear's woman, Liv. Olivia had been forced to spy on Grim Road. Or they'd tried to force her. Fortunately, the woman had a good head on her shoulders and refused to do anything until she had the facts. And the fact was, Bear is as solid as they come.

I led her to Dom's office and knocked on the door. It was open, as usual. He rarely closed his door unless the officers were having a meeting with him. He was working on scouting out a location in town for a clubhouse. We'd never leave our territory here, but Rocket had decided that it would be good to have a place in town for us to crash or party so we could interact with the community. Also, if the authorities thought the new place was our clubhouse, they'd leave this place alone.

"What?" he snapped. "Better be fuckin'… good…" He trailed off as he stared at Calista. Then at me.

Then our joined hands.

I knew it was a bad idea. I knew it was. But I grinned at Dom. "Hey man. Brought home a little stray."

Instantly Dom was on his feet, his face a mask of fury. "My daughter is not a fuckin' stray, you son of a bitch." He reached for Calista, pulling the young woman into his arms and away from my hold on her hand. "Don't hold her fuckin' hand either, Ringo. Off fuckin' limits!"

I grinned. "Only if she says so." I winked at Calista when she peeked up from Dom's chest. For a girl who'd never actually met her father, she was surprisingly at ease.

"She ain't gotta say so 'cause I'm sayin' so." Dom pulled back from Calista, framing her face in his hands as he looked down at her, stroking her cheek tenderly with his thumb "What happened, sweetheart? You hurt?"

She shook her head. "Just tired. And dirty." She sighed. "And my ass might hurt where Peckerwood shoved me down."

Dom stilled, stiffening as he gave me a thunderous look. "Peckerwood? Who the fuck's Peckerwood?"

I shrugged. "Redwood. Not sure what happened to start it, but she finished it."

Dom looked down at Calista. "He put his hands on you, baby?"

She looked from Dom to me and back. Then back to me. "I... I don't want to cause any trouble."

"You ain't." I grinned at her. "Better tell 'em, baby girl. He hears it from me, it won't be the good version."

She winced. "Look. It was nothing. I tried to get past him into you guys' territory and he stopped me. I'm sure it was his job. I fell on my ass. Then I kicked him in the balls."

"He shoved you because you almost dislocated

his little finger when he tried to strangle you." I'd probably just signed Redwood's death warrant, but honestly, he deserved it for putting his hands on Calista. I leveled a gaze at her. "Don't gloss over what happened because you're unsure of us right now. We're not automatically going to take the side of one of our members over you." I nodded to Dom. "Your dad never forgot you. He always protected you and your mother from afar as best he could. At least, he has as long as I've known him."

"Ringo, take Calista to my room. I'll meet you there in a few minutes." Dom brushed past me on his way out the door. "Need to have a chat with... Peckerwood."

Much as I wanted to let this play out with Redwood, I didn't think now was the time. He needed to find out what had driven Calista to a compound filled with morally gray men in the middle of the Goddamned night. Then I might kill the little bastard myself.

"Dom, wait." I grabbed his arm and tugged. He tried to shrug me off, but I held on. "How about you find out what made her come looking for you? 'Cause I'm bettin' whoever it is needs to die before Redwood. That little prick ain't goin' nowhere."

Dom gave me an irritated look before turning back to Calista. "Come here, honey." Dom reached for her again, and Calista went to him willingly.

"Dominic..."

"Yeah, honey." Dom wrapped his arms so tightly around her, she almost disappeared inside them. "I'm so sorry I missed... your life. I did it to protect you, though. You and Tina."

"She taught me how to find you when I was just a child. She made up a silly song and I've sung it all my life. As long as I can remember."

Dom chuckled. "Tina was always so creative. That doesn't surprise me."

"She only told me what the song really meant not long before she died. When she did, it was like everything clicked into place in my brain. She taught me how to use a compass and a map. She even drew one." Calista handed Dom an old silver compass. Looked like it was probably fifty years old.

Dom took it from her, reluctantly letting her out of his embrace. He looked at the instrument, releasing the cover and revealing a small, folded piece of paper. In careful, precise lines, Tina had drawn Calista a map. She'd given her a wide area in Riviera Beach where she could enter the wildlife reserve. Calista had as much information as she could in the limited space of the paper. It was a miracle Calista had found us and not ended up gator bait.

"See?" I raised an eyebrow at Dom. "Must be somethin' fuckin' bad for her to have taken off here."

Dom sighed. "You're a pain in my ass, Ringo. Always have been."

"Wouldn't be doin' my job if I wasn't."

I followed Dom as he lifted Calista into his arms. The girl looked like she was running on adrenaline, from which she was experiencing a massive let down. I had no doubt Dom could see her fatigue as easily as I could.

Oddly, I found myself jealous of the other man. I wanted her to be in *my* arms. Which was all kinds of crazy. The last thing I needed in my life was a woman. Especially one as spirited as this one. I'd given Rocket enough grief when he'd taken Lemon as his woman. Or, rather, when she'd claimed him as her man. I could see how this could end badly for me if I even thought about trying to make Calista mine.

Dom stopped at the door to his room. I stepped forward and opened it. When he took Calista inside, I tried to move in behind him, but Dom just turned and blocked my path.

"Where the fuck do you think you're goin'?"

"Where's it look like I'm goin'?" I loved baiting Dom. I could be as vicious as the next guy -- and I would rain hell down on Redwood when I took care of the bigger problem -- but my job was grim enough without baiting a friend now and then for a laugh. This time, however, I needed to hear what Calista had to say so I could better understand the best way to carry out whatever order Dom was going to give afterward.

"I'm talkin' to my daughter. I don't need you here for that."

"You know I have to be here. There's no need for her to have to repeat herself. We do it all at once where you and I can both be on the same page."

Dom glared at me. "Thought I was sergeant at arms. Meaning I'm actually the boss of you. Not the other way around."

I grinned. "I let you think that." Then I shouldered my way in and shut the door as Dom carried Calista to the couch. He set her down, then snagged a blanket and draped it around her shoulders.

She looked at me. Clear blue eyes gave me a longing look. It wasn't sexual attraction, though I thought I saw that too. It was more like she wanted me for something other than sex. I was a big bastard. My size had always stood me well as enforcer of the club. Given that Calista had basically run blind over some pretty dangerous land in the middle of the night, I was going with her wanting my protection.

Dom dug his phone out of his back pocket and

shot off a text. "Gettin' some breakfast up here as well as something other than beer for the fridge," he muttered. "I'll have Rocket bring clothes and shit."

"Why not ask Lemon? She'll come closer to havin' woman shit than Rocket." I knew why. I was doing this to put Calista more at ease. Dom's eyes narrowed in confusion for a brief moment before he figured out what I was doing.

He snorted. "Right. I'm gonna get the vice president of this club to do something because a woman would be better suited for it. I'm telling my president so he can tell his old lady, who happens to be the vice president, to do something a woman would be more suited to." Dom grinned. "I ain't stupid, boy."

"Your vice president is a woman?" Calista's expression was wide-eyed and curious all at the same time.

"Honey, not just a woman. Lemon is more like a force of nature." I smiled at her. "And there ain't no one in this club I'd rather have by my side. If you're unsure about Dom or me or anyone else in this club, you take it to Lemon. She will have your back."

"But she doesn't know me." Calista looked from Dom to me.

I shrugged. "You're Dom's daughter. That makes you family."

Before she could say anything, there was a knock at the door. Dom crossed to open it, and Lemon stepped inside with Rocket after her.

"What the Christ, Dom?" Lemon stomped inside. "Oh. And don't worry. I already chewed Byte's ass. I'll do the same with Crush when I find him." She pointed at Dom with an accusing finger. "Not cool."

Dom scrubbed a hand over his face. "Never thought I'd ever actually meet her, Lemon. Besides, she's here now." He shrugged. "Now you know."

Lemon glared at Dom before marching straight to Calista and setting a box on the couch next to her. She gave Calista a bright smile. "I'm Lemon, vice president of Grim Road and Rocket's old lady." She hiked a thumb at the president who nodded at Calista. "Byte told Apple who you are and that you were here, so I had time to get you a few things. I'll come by later tonight after you've had a chance to get some rest, and we'll bring you some more shit."

Calista just gaped at Lemon before abruptly snapping her mouth shut. She bit her bottom lip, her gaze going to me once again. I just grinned.

"Thank you so much, Lemon. I-I'll pay you back."

Exasperation crossed Lemon's face. "If I'd wanted you to pay for this shit, I'd have asked before gettin' any of it. Besides, this is all stuff me and Apple put together on the fly. Once the other old ladies are up and at it, the real shopping'll begin. And you still won't fuckin' pay us back."

That seemed to be all Calista could take. Her breathing grew rapid and her eyes glistened. Then she burst into tears.

Chapter Three

Calista

I had no idea where all these emotions came from, but I guess it was only to be expected. I'd been scared out of my mind most of the night. Uncomfortable and in pain, I guess my nerves had taken all the hits they could.

"I'm s-sorry," I sobbed out. Someone had their arms around me, and I had my fists bunched in that same person's T-shirt. And I had no idea who had me.

"Christ," someone swore. "When I find out what sent her here, someone's gonna fuckin' die. Hard."

"Permission granted, Dom," Lemon said cheerfully. "Let me know when all the arrangements are made, and I'll join the effort."

"I'm here! I'm here!"

I heard another woman enter the room and I tried to pull myself together. A big hand rubbed up and down my back as I continued to sob. The feel of those arms tight around me was the only thing that kept me grounded. Even through my tears, the tighter I was held, the better I felt. It wasn't enough to make the fucking tears stop, but it was safe. I guess I needed safe right now, so I could get everything out before dealing with the next set of problems.

There was silence then, "What'd you guys do to her? Lemon?"

"I think it all hit her, Apple," the deep voice rumbled all around me, vibrating through my body and, for some reason, it brought me comfort. I wasn't sure how or why, but my body relaxed even as I knew I was in so much trouble as to not even be believed. Because the man whose arms I was in wasn't my dad. It was Ringo. "Just give her a few minutes. She's good."

"You've got your few minutes." Dom's voice was gruff and cold, deadly. "But only because she seems OK with you. When she's calmed down, we get this all sorted out, and I no longer need you? I'mma kill you for touchin' my daughter."

OK, that surprised me. Enough to pull me back to reality and the moment. I rubbed my cheek against Ringo's chest, even knowing I was a mess. The feel of his hard muscles beneath his shirt was more comforting than I was ready to admit.

A tissue was dangled in front of my face and I took it, blowing my nose. I still had my face against Ringo's chest, unable to put distance between us. I had no idea why. Sure, Ringo had been nice. He'd been the one to sort out who I was and take me to my father. But I had no reason to latch on to him the way I had. Especially knowing my father wasn't pleased. The last thing I wanted to do was to get on Dom's bad side. I needed him if I was going to survive.

"I'm sorry," I croaked, trying to push away from Ringo, but his hold on me didn't ease up.

"Just relax," he murmured. "You're not ready to get up yet." He spoke softly to me, cupping my head to his chest.

"I don't want to c-cause problems."

"You ain't causin' problems, baby girl."

"Don't call her that, you bastard." Dom smacked Ringo on the back of the head.

"Jesus, Dom," Lemon drawled. "Why don't you just piss on her and mark your territory?"

"Lemon…" Dom growled at the vice president but as I looked his way, I saw his gaze shift from Lemon to Rocket. Rocket moved closer to Lemon, draping his arm around her shoulders, standing in solidarity with his vice president and raising an eyebrow. Dom's frustration was more than obvious. "Come on, Rocket! This is my daughter we're talkin' about here! Ringo has no right to touch her. At all, but especially now. She's upset and doesn't know what she's doing."

* * *

Ringo

"That's true," Lemon agreed. "But it doesn't look to me like Calista objects to him touching her right now. In fact, she's clinging to him as hard as he's holdin' her. She's over eighteen. Yes?"

It took everything in my being not to smirk at my SAA. I'd never go against a man when it came to his daughter, but I loved yanking Dom's chain. Besides, Lemon was right. Calista still clung to me. I didn't want to take away her security just yet. It didn't feel right.

What did feel right was having her in my arms and being able to comfort her after whatever she'd just gone through. Which, once I found out what it was, I intended to take care of. Permanently.

Dom sighed, looking no less frustrated or angry. "Yeah. So?"

"Then she has the right to sit with who she wants. If she knees him in the balls like she did Redwood, you can do your worst."

Byte had obviously alerted Rocket and Lemon to the full situation at hand. Which made sense. Lemon liked to sleep in, and she was showing her displeasure at being up at stupid o'clock with snark.

"How has Rocket not smothered you in your sleep, woman?" Dom's muttered response was met with a thunderous look from Rocket.

"Now, now, Dom." Lemon clicked her tongue, *tsking* like Dom was a naughty child. "That's no way to talk about your VP. Rocket wouldn't even think about smothering me in my sleep because he knows I'm irreplaceable." Then she gave Rocket a lascivious grin. "Besides, we have too much fun at night to sleep much."

Not for the first time, I found myself in awe of the young vice president of Grim Road. Lemon had better insight than any person I'd ever met and could read people better than most of the men in the compound.

While I have no doubt Lemon meant every word she'd said, her comments served two purposes. First, it snapped Rocket out of what was about to be a permanent retirement of his sergeant at arms. Second, she let Dom and Calista know in no uncertain terms Lemon was on Calista's side over anyone else. Including Dom's or mine.

"All right." Dom exhaled sharply, as if reaching a resolution within himself. "But this ain't over, Ringo. We're gonna have a long talk later, me and you."

I just grunted, continuing to rub my hand up and down Calista's back.

She shifted in my arms so she could see Dom. "I'm sorry. I didn't want to cause you problems. Mom just told me that if I ever got into trouble, I needed to come find you. Then there was the trouble with Peckerwood at the gate and Ringo helped me."

"You listen to me, honey." Dom knelt down down and reached out to brush a lock of hair that had escaped Calista's bun off her cheek. "You did exactly what you should have done. It was why I gave your mother the location of our compound in the first place. I helped her draw that fuckin' map, baby. So you could find me if you ever needed me." He stroked her cheek tenderly. "You could never cause me problems by coming to me. These guys are just givin' me shit 'cause I'm a protective bastard." He grinned. "And Redwood is gonna wish he'd never laid a hand on you."

She looked horrified, which just made Dom grin wider. "Please don't hurt anyone on my account. He didn't know and was just trying to do his job. He was guarding the gate. Right?"

Dom nodded. "He was, baby. But he should have brought you straight to me as soon as you told him who you were."

"But I didn't." She reached out and took Dom's hand, gripping his fingers tightly. "I didn't tell him. Not until Ringo got there. I didn't want to say anything other than Tina had sent me." She held out the compass she'd been gripping tightly in her fist. "She said to show you this, and you'd know it was me."

Carefully, as if handling the most precious thing in the world, Dom opened his hand to look down at the compass Calista had given him earlier. He caught the small map fluttering to the ground when it slipped from his fingers. A pained expression of longing and sorrow crossed his face before he folded the map and secured it back inside the device and flipped it over. Using the edge of his nail, he pried the back cover off.

Calista let out a small, pained noise but said nothing else. I brushed my lips over her hair for comfort. The scent of woods and moss was sharp but underneath I could smell the sweet essence of her. There were no perfumes or fancy soaps. Just exhausted woman. Made me want to carry her to my room and keep everyone out until she'd eaten, rested, and showered. In that order.

"Easy, honey," I murmured to her. "Let him

look."

Inside was a small card. Calista sat up and leaned in to see. Dom brushed his thumb over the paper, and I saw it was actually a picture. Calista gave a small gasp and her gaze met Dom's. Dom handed her the picture, and I looked over Calista's shoulder as she studied the image.

"That's Mom," she whispered. "With you?"

Dom sighed, swallowing back emotion I couldn't read. "Yeah. We were barely more than teenagers. I remember when that picture was taken." The muscle in Dom's jaw bunched. It was obvious he was struggling for control.

"Maybe we should leave and give them some privacy." Apple spoke softly, tapping Rocket on the shoulder. "Take the guys. Me and Lemon can stay until Calista feels comfortable, but I think they need some time to talk."

Rocket nodded, leaning in to kiss Lemon's temple. "She needs anything, you girls call me. Ringo, when you guys find out what happened, let me know. We'll decide what needs to happen next."

I nodded at my president. I liked that he assumed I wouldn't be leaving. Because I wasn't. I was going to find out what happened to send this girl scrambling through gator-infested wetlands and woodlands at night to find a man she'd never met and had no reason to believe he even knew she existed, other than what her mother had told her.

"I'm the sergeant at arms, Ringo," Dom said, his voice husky with what I was sure was emotion. "When the safety of the club is involved, I decide what has to happen. Not Rocket."

"And I'm the president, Dom. Every decision regarding this club is ultimately mine." Rocket pinned

Dom with a hard gaze. "You're too close. You can be present and help us plan or anything else you feel like you need to do inside the compound to help us prepare. You will not be part of anything going down."

For a moment, I thought Dom was going to protest, but he finally let out a breath and nodded. "Last thing I want to do is something to bring the club under scrutiny." He scrubbed a hand over his face. "Sorry, man."

"Dumbass." Lemon snorted. "Ain't worried about you doin' somethin' to harm the club. You'd never do that. We're worried about *you*. Killin' is one thing. But you shouldn't do it when emotions are high. Not unless it's life or death." She gave Dom a stern look. Like a mother scolding a child. "You kill when you're calm and can properly appreciate the pain and suffering you're inflicting without that haze of anger."

That got a bark of laughter from Calista. She sat up straighter and grinned at Lemon. "I think you and me are gonna be good friends."

Chapter Four

Calista

My mom was right. These people *had* welcomed me. Dominic hadn't rejected me. In fact, I thought he might be a solid wall between me and anything my stepfather could throw at me. And, God help me, there was Ringo.

The very last thing I wanted was to come between him and my father. It seemed like they had a close relationship, though I could be wrong. Unfortunately, I couldn't seem to make myself crawl off Ringo's lap and out of his arms. I was tired, hungry, and feeling extremely vulnerable. Ringo made me feel safe like I hadn't felt since Mom married Borris.

After Rocket and the other men left and shut the door, Dom held out his hand to me. "You're safe here, Calista. No matter what. Understand?"

I put my hand in his, letting him trap it between both of his. "Yes. I-I think I do."

Dom smiled kindly at me, but when I looked deeper, his eyes were cold and flat. There was a chilling rage simmering just beneath the surface, and I wasn't sure if he was angry at me or the whole situation.

"Rein it in, Dom." Ringo spoke softly but with a warning edge. "She doesn't understand us or the club. Not yet. You don't want to come on too strong."

Dom closed his eyes, giving a slight nod. When he looked at me again, there was genuine sorrow and regret shining in his gray eyes. "I never wanted to leave you or your mother, Calista. I didn't even know about you until right before you were born. If I had, I'd've insisted Tina come here to live."

"What happened?" My question was so soft I

wasn't sure if he'd heard me or not. "Why did you leave my mom?"

"To keep her safe." Dom sighed, squeezing my hand once before letting go and moving back to his chair. He sprawled out with his legs in front of him, crossed at the ankles as he scrubbed a hand over his face several times. "We hadn't known each other long, but she was my world from the moment we met. We were only together a couple of months before I left. Had my life not gone to hell and back, I'm sure we'd've still been together." He snorted. "I mean, I gave her the location of this place. That should tell anyone here all they need to know. So, baby, I've not been in your life as your father, but I will be now as much as you want me. I will protect you and use the full weight of my position in this club -- which is just as much as Rocket's or Lemon's because I'm in charge of safety -- to slay your demons. So I need to know what sent you running to me."

It wasn't a question. It also wasn't something I'd ever refuse to give him. He deserved to know why I came, though, and caused chaos in his club. That had never been my intent.

"Mom died a few years ago," I began.

"Yeah, baby. Had Byte keeping an eye on both of you. Discreetly and only the surface of your lives, so he didn't go too in-depth, but I knew when she passed."

"Then you might know more than me. We were told it was an aggressive form of some kind of blood cancer, but my mom didn't think so."

Dom tilted his head, narrowing his eyes. "Oh?"

"Yeah. She thought she'd been poisoned. The last few days, she refused to eat or drink anything I didn't bring her. That's when she told me the meaning of the song she'd taught me when I was little and gave me the compass." I nearly sobbed in grief. "Mom and I were always really tight. The only argument we ever had was when she accepted Borris Illivitch's marriage proposal."

"You didn't want her to marry?" Dom raised an eyebrow, like he didn't think that was the whole story. He was right.

"No. It wasn't that. I didn't want her to marry Borris. He's a swine."

Dom gave me a small smile, but I could see he understood. "Did she love him?" Did I imagine he winced when he asked that question?

"No. And what I'm going to say next is strictly the truth as I see it, Dom, but I don't think Mom ever loved anyone in her life other than me. And you."

Yeah. That went over about as well as I expected. Dom sucked in a breath, then stood to pace the room. There was no way my mom would have fallen for someone who didn't love her back. Dom had loved my mom.

"Christ," he muttered, pausing to lean against a wall. He thumped his head a few times before turning back to me. "Why? Why did she marry Illivitch." It wasn't a demand phrased as a question, but I was under no illusion he would accept it if I refused to answer. So I evaded a little bit. "You said you had someone watching her. Did he not tell you?"

"I said he didn't dig deep. He just made sure you guys weren't in any immediate danger and only checked up once a month or so. He said if there was anything major, he had alarms in place that would notify him. Which is how I knew Tina was ill. Though he only found out a couple days before she died."

"Then he found out the same time we did. Mom demanded to be brought back to the house to spend whatever time she had left. In reality, it was where she'd hidden the compass, and she wanted to make sure I got it before she passed."

"Answer me, honey," Dom demanded. I could see pain in his eyes, and it made me reach out to him when I still didn't want to leave the safety of Ringo's embrace.

I moved from Ringo's lap -- which I'd probably be mortified about later -- and crossed to my dad. "We were living on the streets. Mom couldn't get a job and I wasn't old enough. We both took odd jobs that paid cash so we had enough money to eat, but it was a struggle. Then she met Borris Illivitch." I tried to keep the bitterness out of my voice but wasn't sure how well I managed. "He seemed like a Godsend, though there were red flags from the beginning."

"Did he hurt either of you?"

I took a deep breath, then let it out. "Not... directly. He was always kind to my mother, on the surface at least. There was always something that was a little bit off about him."

"What does 'not directly' mean?" Any tenderness Dom might have had was turned off now. It was clear he had an issue with the way I'd phrased my answer.

"Well, once they became involved, he wouldn't let my mother work. Or me. And he kept us both practically on lockdown. I was homeschooled. He *said* by the best educators money could buy."

"He said?"

"Yeah. I tested out for my GED when I turned sixteen and that was the end of my education. After that, everything I learned was about social niceties. What was expected of me in the company of anyone Borris wanted to introduce to me. And neither me nor my mother had any friends Borris didn't approve of. Which is to say no one outside his circle." I knew I sounded bitter, but I could also hear the fear in my voice I tried so hard to hide. "He's not going to just let me go, Dom."

There was a long silence where I wasn't sure anyone was even breathing. I could see Dom working things out in his head. I even saw the exact moment he realized what Illivitch had done to my mother and me and shook his head to deny those conclusions. Ringo, however, wasn't as restrained.

"Oh, *hell* no! He was grooming you? He was selling you to someone?"

I winced. "When you put it like that..."

"Did he mention anything like this before your mother died?" Dom ignored Ringo's outburst, which was probably a good thing at the moment.

"No. But she knew. Or suspected. She tried to get us out of there. Even had plans in place to make our escape. That's when she got sick."

"Imma kill that motherfucker," Ringo said at the same time Dom said, "He's a dead sumbitch."

I thought I should protest. It's what any decent person would do. I must not have been a decent person because I nodded my head. "He's a bad person."

Dom took a breath. "Tell me what happened next."

"Most of it I already told you. She thought she was being poisoned so she refused to see anyone but me. She even refused to see Borris."

"He didn't insist on being with her?" Dom looked thunderous, but also... pained? This hurt him. He really did feel something for my mother.

"I left her side one evening and when I came back the next morning, she was dead. Borris was standing over her. She had her eyes open in death and Borris had a satisfied look on his face. I imagined he was thinking it was about fucking time."

"Did he hurt you then?" Dom's voice was hard, but his expression was tightly controlled.

"No. He never hurt me or Mom physically. I mean, unless he actually did poison her or something. I just got the feeling that it was more because we were beneath his notice than any desire to *not* hurt us."

"If he didn't hurt you, why did you take off running through the forest in the middle of the night, hmm?" Dom reached out and cupped the side of my face gently. He smiled down at me with genuine affection, but there was also a desire to really fucking hurt someone shining just as brightly. While I was filled with overwhelming relief that my father wanted me and wasn't angry that I had probably brought danger straight to his door... Well, at least he wasn't angry yet. Instead, he had a strong desire to avenge me in whatever way. To protect me from whatever had terrified me so much I'd risk death to find him.

"I overheard him... selling me. Like I was a prostitute. He told the guy he could do whatever he wanted to me. That since I was..." I stopped, clearing my throat. I was acutely aware of Ringo still sitting on the couch behind me. I wanted to look at him, but it was impossible. My back was to him, and I figured it would be a bad move to take my attention away from my father at the moment.

Taking a deep breath, I continued. "Since I was a virgin, I would cost twice as much, but he was given no limits on what he could do to me." I glanced up at Dom again, not able to hold his gaze. His expression gave nothing away, but there was the slightest crinkle of his forehead and at the corner of his eyes that told me the man was furious. "He... that is, Borris, didn't leave anything to the imagination as to what the guy could do to me. The only restriction was that he wasn't to mark my skin or hit my face. If I died, he'd see the guy died the same way, but otherwise, he gave him free rein to do whatever he wanted to do to me." I could feel my throat closing up, hear my voice breaking on each word. "Everything imaginable to sexually terrorize someone. You know. Like me."

"Do you know who this man was?" Dom's voice was still gentle, but I could see the sweat erupt over his brow. "Who he was giving you to?"

I shook my head. "Only that my stepfather owed him a lot of money. Whatever the amount, I was supposed to wipe the slate clean. I think it was a loan, but I could have remembered wrong. I wasn't exactly thinking clearly."

"You don't live in Riviera Beach." Dom narrowed his eyes at me. Did he not believe me? If this turned bad, would he kill me?

"No. We live in Miami. This was the requested drop-off place by the buyer. But it's why I waited to try and get away until we were here. I knew this was where I needed to be." I shrugged. "I thought it would keep my chances of living through this higher than having to travel from Miami to Riviera Beach."

"Yes. You thought right." Whatever Dom was thinking he was holding tight, leaving me a bit uneasy.

Dom glanced over my head. "Ringo, I need to reach out to El Segador." His expression hardened, all the sergeant at arms of his club now. "To do that, I've got to talk with Rocket and Lemon." He stabbed a finger in Ringo's direction. "You keep her safe and comfortable. And if your dick touches her anywhere, I'll cut it off and feed it to you."

Chapter Five

Ringo

"You keep her safe and comfortable. And if your dick touches her anywhere, I'll cut it off and feed it to you."

Yeah. I got it. Dom wasn't OK with me being with his daughter. I mean, I was pretty sure I could get around him cutting off my dick by the mere fact he'd never willingly touch my dick, but I'd never take advantage of any woman in Calista's position. Especially not this one. Not only was she my MC brother's daughter, but she was special.

I wasn't too proud to admit I was taken with her. I wasn't sure why, but she'd snagged my attention and wouldn't let go. Even now, I itched to pull her back into my arms to comfort her. It was where she belonged. And that wasn't me. I didn't claim women. Not like I wanted to claim Calista. No, I didn't know her. All I knew was that she'd braved the wild at night on her own to save herself instead of calmly walking to her fate. Or waiting for someone to rescue her. That alone made her fierce.

Once Dom was gone, Calista sagged against the wall. I could tell she was bone tired.

"Hey, baby girl," I murmured as I stood and stepped toward her. "You've got to be starving. Apple left some stuff on the table. Wanna see what she brought?"

She looked up at me. It was easy to see the exhaustion on her face. "Yeah. I'd like a bath first, though. I've got mud and swamp water all over me." She wrinkled her nose delicately. "I stink."

I chuckled. "Darlin', I don't think you could ever stink. I should know. I carried you here. That's about as close as a person can get." Then I winked at her. "At least with our clothes on."

I had no idea why I said it -- flirting with her wasn't a great idea -- but her smile when I did made me not care so much about what Dom thought.

The beauty of that smile made my breath catch. Instead of the sunrise, I wanted to wake up to this smiling woman every fuckin' day.

Finally, I let my grin fade. She continued to look at me shyly but not like she was embarrassed. Yeah. She was interested. Put the ball decidedly in my favor.

"Come on. These apartments in the main compound are pretty much the same. Let me show you the bathroom, and you can have some privacy. I'll keep breakfast warm for you."

"Thank you, Ringo. Thanks for believing me and bringing me to Dominic. I wasn't sure what I was going to do if I couldn't get in."

"I knew you the second I got a good look at you. Dom showed me pictures of you as soon as he got them. He's always been very proud of you. Broke his heart when he heard about your mother. He wanted to go after you, but he knew Tina had married and that the man you were staying with was the only father you'd ever known. No one turned up anything on Illivitch, but I don't think Crush or Byte dug too deeply. They knew you were safe, at least, at the time. They had measures in place to alert them if you were in extreme danger. But this? If they'd've turned up anything like the selling of young women, they'd have told Rocket and Dom immediately. We'd have come for you."

She shook her head. "I don't understand. None of you know me. Dominic doesn't know me. All he has are pictures sent to him by a dead woman."

"You have the same expressions he does

sometimes," I pointed out. "I saw how you dealt with Redwood. You're your father's daughter. Anyone not blind can see it."

She nodded at me once. "Thank you. If my mom was to be believed and not just giving me a reason to *not* hate him, Dominic was always a brave man, serving his country and protecting all of us."

"That pretty much sums up Dom. Though, he no longer works for the government officially." I shrugged. "Once a SEAL, always a SEAL."

She nodded again, then disappeared into the bathroom.

I leaned back against the wall. It was all I could do to keep my legs underneath me. This girl had the power to bring me to my knees with a fucking *look*. "God, I'm so fucked," I muttered to myself.

With a grunt, I moved to the table to check out what the women had brought up. Leftover brisket, potato salad, baked beans, and biscuits. There was an assortment of fruits and a vegetable tray, both with dip. They'd also brought a single cup coffeepot as well as an assortment of juices and sodas. Of course, Dom already had beer. No coffee pot of his own, but a whole fridge full of beer. I found it amusing the women knew this about Dom and came prepared.

I put the warm dishes in the oven on a low temperature, just to keep it all warm until she was ready to come out.

Twenty minutes later, she did. She was dressed in men's lounge pants and a T-shirt, both of which looked all too familiar. The sight of her in my clothes was a little bit more than I could bear. Because all I could think about now was stripping them off her. How the fuck Lemon ended up bringing my clothes I had no idea, but I was sure it was a conspiracy.

The shirt came down to mid-thigh and slid off one slim shoulder. She wasn't wearing a bra that I could tell. She was slight and my shirt was at least four or five sizes too big, but there was no strap over that creamy shoulder. I was pretty sure I saw a nipple tenting the cotton when she moved. Though the pants were several sizes too big, she'd rolled up the bottoms so they clung to her ankles. Her hair was wet, but she brushed out what I now saw were long, curly strands of silk that rolled gently down her back to the curve of her ass.

"Sweet Jesus." I must have whispered it out loud because Calista stopped and looked in my direction. I scrubbed a hand over my mouth. Try as I might, though, I couldn't look away from her. There was nothing remotely sexy about the way she looked, but I'll be Goddamned if my dick wasn't hard as a motherfucker now.

She studied me for a moment, then took a careful step toward the table, never taking her eyes off me. I probably looked exactly like what I was: a predator who'd found his prey.

Calista sat at the table and picked up the bottle of water I'd left out and removed the cap. Never taking her eyes from me, she took a long pull... Until her thirst overrode her trepidation.

The water was cold and, even though I knew she'd likely drunk while she was in the bathroom, there was nothing quite like an ice-cold bottle of water to quench a thirst. Her eyes slipped shut, and she groaned as she gulped down the water.

"Christ," I muttered again. "You're gonna be the death of me, baby girl."

I went to the oven and took out the food Apple had brought, setting everything on the table. "I know it's not breakfast food, but it's something." I got the fruit and veggies out of the fridge, too. "If there isn't anything here you want, I'll go down and snag some breakfast. Apple's made it her mission to feed everyone while she's here and, I have to admit, the girl ain't a bad cook."

Calista gave me a small smile. "This all looks wonderful. Don't let me forget to thank whoever made and brought this up."

"That'd be Apple again. And don't worry. I'm sure they'll all be back later. Right now, though, you need food and rest."

"What's going to happen next?" She met my gaze and for the first time, she looked haunted.

"Nothin' you need to worry about, baby girl. Let your daddy take care of everything. It's what he does."

"I brought these problems straight to him. I should help."

"You are. By staying here and lettin' him do this." I sat down next to her and gripped her hand in a tight squeeze. Immediately, pleasure zinged through my hand up my body and went straight to my cock. I had to get a handle on this! If Dom walked in and saw me sporting the mother of all hard-ons he would *not* be impressed.

I cleared my throat and forced myself to let her go. Then the woman had to go and turn her hand so she grabbed onto my fingers. Our gazes clashed. Her breathing sped up until a small sob escaped her.

She let go of my hand, but I wasn't having that. Everything inside me screamed to comfort her in any way she needed. Right now, I thought she just needed to feel safe again.

"Talk to me, honey. Tell me what you need."

With a heart-wrenching sob, she stood so fast the

chair fell over backward and she threw herself at me. I caught her, wrapping my arms around her tightly. I urged her onto my lap, draping her legs on either side of my hips. Then I stood with her and walked to the couch to sit.

Calista clung so tightly she nearly strangled me, but I wasn't about to make her let up. I just rubbed her back with one hand while the other arm was around her, holding her tightly to me.

Of course, Dom chose that moment to come back. "Christ, Ringo," he growled. "I'm gonna hate it, but when she's feeling safe and more like herself, you know I'm going to have to kill you. Right?"

"Yeah, brother. I hear you." I didn't stop, though. If this woman needed, I provided. Even if providing for her meant taking a beating from her old man. It was scary really. How far gone I was on this woman already. Hell, the only thing I knew about her was that she was brave beyond measure. Kind of like Lemon. Which... Yeah. I wasn't thinkin' about that one. I wasn't sure I was man enough to endure that kind of a woman. But, by God, I was going to try. And just like that, I knew Calista was going to be mine.

Calista stirred then, wiping her nose on the back of her wrist with a grimace. "You can't kill him, Dom," she said in a soft voice. "I jumped him. Not the other way around." Then she stiffened, moving from my lap to the floor. I shot Dom an annoyed look. It was his fault she was trying to raise her shields again.

"He's not really gonna kill me, baby girl." I used the nickname deliberately, needing Dom to see he could threaten, could even follow through with those threats, but he was not going to intimidate me into staying away from Calista. She was his daughter, but she'd chosen me as her protector. That was very clear.

"Don't bet on it," Dom grumbled. "Baby." He reached for Calista. She was hesitant, but went to him. He pulled her into a loose embrace. He still almost completely enveloped her with his much larger frame. Calista allowed the show of affection and returned it, but she didn't relax. It was more like she was doing something she felt like she was expected to do.

"I'm gonna get those fuckers for you, honey. You'll be safe and can do anything or go anywhere you want without thinkin' they'll be on your tail."

"I don't..." Her voice broke. "I don't have anywhere to go."

"Then you stay here. Hell, I'd have suggested that first, but I didn't want to freak you out. I'm much rather have you here where Lemon and Apple can get you into all kinds of mischief than have you by yourself in the city."

Calista glanced in my direction before ducking her head. "It's really OK if I stay here? Even after I kicked Peckerwood in the balls?"

"Yeah, honey. Maybe even *because* you busted his balls. Means you can hold your own with the men in this outfit." He gave me a hard stare. "Any of 'em come on to you, I want to know about it."

"I'm sure no one will do that," she said softly, her gaze flickered to me several times.

"Hey." I winked at her. "I'll be comin' on to you. But don't worry. It'll be our secret."

To my surprise -- and to Dom's if the expression on his face was any indication -- Calista let out a small giggle before clapping her hand over her mouth. Christ! The woman was a combination of hardass and innocence. How the fuck was I supposed to resist that?

Dom grumbled under his breath. "I suppose this is why Tina didn't want me in your life. She knew I'd smother any girl child I had to within an inch of her life."

Calista shook her head, amusement still on her face. "Actually, she told me she would have loved watching you interact with me. Said you'd have run off any boy I tried to date and would probably forbid me from dating until I was forty. And only then because you'd be too old to prevent it."

"Oh, make no mistake, honey. You want to date when you're forty, I might be going downhill in the fitness department, but I'll still be able to pick up a gun and shoot with complete accuracy." Dom said this as a reflex. By the time he finished, there was a look of abject horror on his face and Calista was grinning like a loon.

"Looks like Mom was right."

"Ah, hell." Dom laced his fingers behind his head and closed his eyes, taking a deep breath. When he looked up again, there was a soft expression on his face. One I'd never seen on the big bruiser before. If this is what having kids did to a man, I wasn't really sure I wanted to go down that rabbit hole. Which, I knew, is where I was headed. "I'm sorry, Calista," he said, sounding very contrite. "But I just can't stand by and watch you date that one over there." He nodded in my direction. "He's fuckin' Army." He said that last word like it left a bitter taste in his mouth. "Now, if he were Navy, or even Marine, I might be able to tolerate the thought. Not sayin' I'd let him date you, just that he might get to live if he tried. But a fuckin' Bullet Catcher? Ain't fuckin' happenin', baby."

That really got the giggles from Calista.

"Hey," I said. "We all know Joe's are better'n Jarheads."

The banter between me and Dom seemed to

defuse most of the tension. At least, Calista's shoulders were more relaxed, and she no longer looked like she was afraid of stepping a toe out of line.

"No one said I was dating anyone," she said primly, but her gaze slid to mine and she ducked her head.

"You're not old enough to date," Dom groused. "You're barely out of your teens."

"Dad, I'm twenty-one." Calista smiled but I could see the exact moment she realized she'd called Dom "Dad." An unsure expression crossed her face before she shut it down, her face going blank.

I gave Dom a hard look, wondering if he'd pick up on it and call her out or simply roll with it. I wasn't sure either one of those options were great.

To my surprise -- and one I'd gleefully relay to Lemon later -- Dom sucked in a breath, his eyes filling with tears. The big, bad sergeant at arms for one of the most feared group of men in the world, sank to his knees in front of Calista and wrapped his arms around her waist, burying his face into her abdomen and sobbed like his heart was breaking.

Chapter Six

Calista

No one was more startled than me when I called Dominic "Dad." It was really only a matter of time before I slipped up anyway. My mother always referred to him as my dad, so I'd always thought of him that way. I'd tried not to let that little girl who desperately wanted a father figure to protect and love her out for anyone to see. Even my mother when she'd been alive. The last thing I'd ever wanted to do was make her feel like she'd failed at giving me something I needed. It was because we were in such a desperate situation that she'd taken up with Borris in the first place. He was much older than my mother and told her he needed a caregiver in his elder days and that in exchange for her being his wife, he'd make sure I had everything I needed. I was beginning to think the reality was something far different, but I wasn't about to say so. If these men found confirmation of what I suspected, then I'd believe them. But I wasn't throwing it out there.

Now, Dom was on his knees in front of me, sobbing like his heart was breaking. I wasn't sure what to do. I threaded one hand through his hair and held him to me, while patting his shoulder with the other and just... let him get it all out. Truth be told, I was close to tears my own damn self.

It took a couple of minutes, but Dom cleared his throat and stood. Picking me up in his arms, he carried me to the chair next to the couch where Ringo still sat, cradling me in his lap. I wasn't as comfortable with him as I was with Ringo, but I knew I could get there. I didn't know this man. Had never even seen a picture of him. Mom had said it was for safety reasons. The thought that there was a picture of him and Mom in that compass and I hadn't known -- that my mom might not have known -- was the thing I clung to. Dom had given her that compass never intending to come back to her, but not wanting her to forget him. Maybe? There were so many questions I had, and I wasn't sure I was brave enough to ask them.

"This compound is full of men some people in the U.S. government would love to be rid of. Everyone here had done some things that might not have been sanctioned by the government at the time but ordered done just the same."

"Are you talking about something like... I don't know. Black Ops?"

"That's exactly what I'm talking about."

"I thought that was only in the movies. Like *for real.*"

Dom grinned down at his daughter. "No, honey. It's not as glamorous as it is in the movies, but one thing they got right is that, if something goes wrong or they decide what they ordered you to do was wrong, you're a liability. Not all of us'd be in trouble if anyone knew we were still alive and kickin', but there are several who'd be hunted down and shot on sight."

"And by telling me this, do I have to stay here now?"

Again, Dom grinned. "Nope. I'm tellin' you this because I want you in my life. However I can have you. That means I have to give you my trust to earn yours. So there it is. I just gave you the key to bring us all down."

I sucked in a breath, shaking my head. "I don't want that."

"I know, honey. I did it anyway. Because I'm all in with you. The way I should have been with your mother."

"But you left her to keep her safe." I could feel tears pricking my eyes. Only fitting since he'd cried in front of me when I'd have bet my life he wasn't a man who ever cried in front of others. Hell, he probably didn't let himself feel emotion strongly enough to have the need to cry.

"Yeah, but I should have known no one could keep her as safe as I could. It's not a mistake I'm makin' again. Not with you, Calista." He glanced up at me, raising an eyebrow. "Which is why, if you stay, I want my enforcer here, Ringo, to claim you."

I started, pushing away from him slightly. Dom didn't try to hold me, but kept his arms loosely around me, as if reluctant to let me up. Shaking my head, I gasped out, "You can't be serious."

Dom looked from me to Ringo and back. "You tellin' me you don't want it to be him? You want to check out some of the other guys here? See if one fits?"

"I don't need to be claimed by anyone." It was a token protest at best, and I was woman enough to admit it. At least to myself. The thought of being thrown together with Ringo was more of a turn on than I wanted to admit. I already felt safe with him. Hell, I wanted to have him near more than I wanted Dom. Dom was my father, but the fact was, I'd known Ringo longer. Maybe only a couple minutes longer, but still!

Dom grinned at me. "Well, it's the only way I'm lettin' you be near him. He's interested in you and I'm keeping him honest."

"Huh?" I looked back at Ringo, who had the biggest shit-eating grin on his face I'd ever seen. "Are the two of you making fun of me?" Because if they were, I'd never forgive them. Or myself for such poor judgment.

"Not at all, honey," Dom said, giving me a kind look. "I just want you safe." He shot me a wry look. "Much as I hate to admit it, the smug bastard would be the best protection for you. He's ruthless and deadly, but he's got a good heart."

"Wow, bro," Ringo drawled as he put his arms across the back of the couch, crossing one ankle over the opposite knee. "Didn't know you cared."

"I don't," Dom snapped, looking as disgruntled as a man could. "And I'll never repeat what I said to anyone outside this room. You're still a dumbass, and I'll still give you hell every chance I get."

Again, I studied both men. "I'm not sure about this. I don't want to be a burden or forced on anyone. And I most certainly don't want to run from one monster straight to another." I shook my head, though, in my heart, I knew what Dom proposed wasn't anything like what Borris had.

"Calista," Dom whispered, brokenly. "No. No one would ever force you into something like that. Least of all me. I only want you protected. You like Ringo. He likes you." He shrugged, shaking his head. "It's just our way. Our men know almost at first sight when they find the woman they want. I don't think Ringo's any different."

"What about you?" I couldn't help the question. It felt like a low blow, but I had to know. "Did you want my mom for something more than a passing fling?"

Dom lowered his head, then leaned back to stare at the ceiling, his head resting on the back of the chair. "Yeah, honey. I did. I intended to marry her, then my life went all to shit and back. The last time I met up with her was when I made her memorize the map to this place from Riviera Beach. I spent the entire night with her. Makin' sure she never forgot the directions. Or me." A small smile parted his lips as he continued to look at the ceiling. "God, I loved her..." His voice was nearly a whisper now. "I had to keep her safe and the only way to do that was to leave her alone. I admit, I was hurt she gave in as easily as she did. Looking back, she probably knew she was pregnant, was afraid to be near me, and used my lesson as the excuse she needed to forget I existed. Lord knew I scared her half to death to make an impression on her. I wanted her with me more than anything other than wanting to keep her safe. So I didn't push her. Thinkin' now that was the exact wrong thing to do."

"You were just trying to do what you thought was right." I found myself believing my words. They weren't just something I was saying to make him -- and myself -- feel better. Dom was exactly the type of man to sacrifice himself to keep his family safe. I sighed. "What if we hate each other?"

"Then I kick his ass and he changes his attitude." I thought he was only half joking.

I turned to study Ringo. He was still draped lazily on the couch. The smirk on his face was sexy as fuck, and I wanted to know what those lips felt like on mine.

"Even if it looks like Dom's just selling you to the highest bidder, you know this is different." Ringo's expression was deceptive. On the one hand, he looked relaxed and arrogant. But, underneath the surface, there was a vulnerability he tried to bury deep. I had to really study him to see even a glimmer. It was there, though. The expectation that I'd reject him.

'Course, I didn't know the guy. Maybe I was reading way more into it than I should.

Lord knew refusing this would be the smart thing to do. Unfortunately, I'd never been accused of being smart.

"Maybe," I conceded. "I still think I should have the choice to not be claimed by anyone."

"Sorry, honey," Dom said with a grin. "I want you safe. To ensure that, I want my best man on you. That's Ringo. Sure, he could still do the job and not make any kind of claim on you. But he and I both know that you'll end up sleeping with him." He held up a hand to stave off an argument. "No reflection on either of you. Just saying I can see he's got it for you, and you're certainly interested in him. He wouldn't want other men around you and would turn into a grouch when some of our brothers made a play for you, because he'd still be responsible for your safety and would have to be with you. It would all turn into a ghastly mess. People might even end up dying." Dom looked smug. Like he knew there was no way I'd refuse him. We both knew I'd protest but I'd give in eventually.

Mainly because he was right. If I spent much time in Ringo's presence, if he showed the least bit of interest in me, I'd end up in his bed. I might be a virgin, but I knew that about myself. Besides, I'd rather give myself to a man I wanted -- no matter what happened later -- than have it sold or taken from me.

"If I agree to this, you're not going to kill Ringo. Right?"

Dom barked out a laugh. "No, honey."

"I mean, you threatened to before. And that if his dick touched me you'd cut it off and feed it to him." I pointed an accusing finger at Dom. "I distinctly remember that."

"As long as he treats you right, his dick'll be

safe."

"So what does all this mean? Him claiming me?"

"It means you'll be my old lady. In the eyes of the club, we'd be married. Also means you'll not only have my and Dom's protection, but that of the entire club." He shrugged. "Probably would anyway, but there are a few stubborn old goats who'd resist." He shrugged. "Not that it would matter. Lemon would quash that shit the second it left someone's mouth. But havin' someone claim you makes it all simple."

I leveled a hard gaze on Ringo. "I want one thing perfectly clear before we go any further."

"What's that?" Ringo raised an eyebrow as if to tell me to do my worst.

"If being your old lady is the same as being married, I will accept nothing less than fidelity. I absolutely will not tolerate being cheated on."

"That's part of it, baby girl." Ringo gave me a nod of acknowledgment. "You're mine. I'm yours."

"You break that rule, Ringo, Dom won't have to cut off your dick and feed it to you. I'll shove it up your ass."

Chapter Seven
Ringo

Yeah. I was totally fucked. This woman...

"Sweet Christ," Dom muttered. "Get her shit and get outta here, Ringo. I absolutely will not let you dry hump my daughter in my fuckin' quarters." Then he pointed at Calista. "You. If he hurts you, or doesn't make it good for you --"

"Right. Come see you."

"Actually no. Not unless you want him dead. Go to Lemon. Especially with the latter 'cause I do *not* want to know."

That made Calista burst out laughing. "Point taken."

"Now. Ringo. Take care of my girl. You don't and you will answer to me."

"On it, boss." With a grin, I stood and crossed to Calista. "Why don't you rummage through that box Lemon gave you and find some jeans and socks. Get your boots back on and we'll take my bike." I smirked at Dom, knowing putting his daughter on the back of my bike was probably one more nail in my coffin, but he'd been the one to start this.

It didn't take her long to change. "Where we going?" We walked outside the clubhouse and she glanced over her shoulder like she was really having second thoughts about the whole leaving-with-me thing.

"On a ride around the compound. Thought you might like a little taste of what you're in for."

She stopped dead in her tracks. "This better not be some nefarious way to do something awful. Because you might hurt me, but unless you kill me, you have to sleep sometime. I will totally follow through on my promise to cut off your dick and shove it up your ass."

That got a bark of laughter from me. "Nefarious? Nah. Anything I do to you might be sinful, but I promise you'll enjoy it and beg me for more." I tugged her onward. "I think you'll enjoy the bike. Nothin' like the wind in your hair and a powerful machine between your legs." I gave her my best wicked grin.

Her eyes widened. "Oh, no, you didn't!" But she was grinning and continued on with me without more protest.

I helped her on the bike, showing her where to put her feet. "Do *not* touch the pipes. They will burn you even through thick denim."

She nodded, then I climbed aboard and reached down to start up my bike. The rattle of the pipes always got my blood pumping. Now, with a sexy woman on the back...

No. Scratch that. Not with *a* sexy woman. *My* sexy woman. She was thirteen years younger than me, the daughter of my SAA, and possibly a stronger woman than I was ever prepared for, but I wasn't giving her up.

When she put her hands at my sides, gripping my cut, I gently took one hand and tugged her forward until both of her arms were wrapped around me. One hand was flat against my stomach, while the other one gripped her wrist so she was locked to me. She didn't seem to know how she could touch me so she was tentative, but I pressed my hands over hers, letting her know she could touch me all she wanted. Then we took off.

The compound was completely fenced in on a crap-ton of land. With the sun just now coming up and the heat not so great, I thought she might like a tour around the various sections. Just so she could see the terrain.

We didn't have a road through the place, exactly, but a wide, dirt path packed hard. While I couldn't ride with a great deal of speed, it was a fairly smooth ride. Prospects walked the path two or three times a week to keep the weeds beat back and the trail maintained, especially after rain or in sections we'd had to build wooden trails over.

The longer we rode, the more relaxed Calista became. At one point, I felt her cheek rub up and down my back. I couldn't help but rub her leg as we continued.

It wasn't long before my phone buzzed with a text. We'd just pulled up outside the family section, fifty acres which were fenced off with a privacy fence, so I dug into my back pocket to fish it out. In the process, my hand brushed Calista's inner thigh. Even through our clothes, electricity seemed to arc between us. She shivered and tightened her grip around my waist. I looked back over my shoulder and winked at her. She buried her face in my back, but I saw the excited smile before she turned away from me completely. She still rubbed her face against my back.

I smirked to myself as I looked at the text message.

Lemon: *Gt ur ass hr. 2nd [^] on lt.*

Me: *English please.*

Lemon: *FIO beoch*

Heaven help me.

Turned out she and Apple had gotten the second house on the left ready for us. Whatever.

"Here." Lemon handed Calista a phone. "It's got mine and Apple's numbers programmed into it, as well as Dom, Ringo, and Rocket. Full disclosure: Rocket is mine. I really like you, but if you touch him without permission I'll have to hurt you. I don't want to hurt you, girl. You're gonna join me, Apple, and the other old ladies and we're gonna keep these guys from gettin' completely out of control." Lemon smiled brightly and, to my surprise, Calista laughed, her eyes dancing in merriment.

"Yeah. I think we are."

Apple grinned as she came out of the house. "Everything's ready. Place has been aired out and fresh linens are in the bedrooms and bathrooms. This one has a queen and a full, but there's plenty of room for a king in the master bedroom when you're ready." Apple was the milder sister, but she was still a handful. Especially since coming to Grim Road to live.

It was like, before a point in her life, she was one way. After that point, she was another. She was more abrasive than Lemon. Lemon had learned to joke. Somewhat. Apple meant every cutting barb she threw. And sometimes, she could be vicious. I was glad she was following Lemon's lead in taking care of Calista. Having Apple for an enemy wasn't advisable.

"Thanks, guys." I grinned at both women and, before either knew I was going to, pulled them both into an embrace for a full two seconds before Lemon shrieked, ducking out of my hold. Apple backed up three full steps, looking at me like I'd grown two heads.

"What the fuck? Eww!" Lemon did a little dance, like something had just creeped her the fuck out. "Ringo germs! I'll probably get the bubonic clap! Or a fiery, raging case of hemorrhoids! Bath! I need a bath! And liquor. And pot! OMG! Lots of pot!"

"That was just gross, Ringo." Apple brushed herself off with a frown. Like I'd gotten dog shit on them. Meanwhile, Calista was laughing like a loon, bent double as she guffawed.

I looked appropriately put out with the women as I snagged Calista's hand. "That was cold, y'all."

Lemon pointed at me, pointing to her eyes, then at me a couple of times. All kidding aside, I got the message. She was watching, and I absolutely would not do anything to hurt Calista.

As we entered the house, Calista was still wiping tears from her eyes. "Those women are awesome!" She stood with her back against the door, a huge smile on her face as she laughed. "You did that on purpose."

I snorted. "Right. 'Cause I love setting myself up for ridicule from the tiny tyrants."

"Oh..." Her eyes got wider, and she started laughing again, like this was all the height of hilarity. "You better not let either of them hear you call them that. I have a feeling it won't work out so well for you."

I couldn't help the grin and knew there was likely some soft, goofy expression on my face. How the fuck had I decided I liked soft and sweet? 'Cause this girl was so fucking sweet it was giving me cavities. Her reactions were genuine. She was scared, but brave. She'd had one small meltdown, but I thought she still needed to process everything that had happened tonight.

I let her calm down somewhat. She sat on the couch, plopped down like she was exhausted. Given that she'd been on the run all night, I was sure she was.

"You all right, baby girl?" I moved to the side table where I kept a bottle of Jack. I poured us both a shot, then handed her the glass, crouching in front of her, careful to go slowly so I didn't startle her.

She took the glass and sniffled, tears still leaking from her eyes. There was a smile on her face, but it started to falter. "Well, I'm on the run from my stepfather and whoever he thought he was gonna sell me to. When they catch me, they're going to do things to me I can't even imagine."

She shot the whiskey, sputtering slightly before setting the glass down next to her. I quickly shot mine and set my glass beside hers. She rubbed her hand under her nose to catch a drip. I reached to the side table for a box of tissues someone had thought to bring. Apple, no doubt. She was turning into the hard-ass of the two, but she still had a soft spot. Mostly, when there was someone she thought needed taking care of.

Once Calista'd blown her nose she met my gaze. "I'm sorry I dragged you into this. It's not fair to you and, no matter how attracted I am to you, I don't think I'm ready for this yet."

"For what, baby? Sex?"

She closed her eyes and exhaled, like I was dancing on the very last nerve she had. "Yes, Ringo. Sex. You heard me. I'm a virgin. Can't say I haven't watched porn or anything. I know about all the stuff Borris promised the other guy he could do." She met my gaze again. This time, there was a wealth of emotions shining there. Fear. Curiosity. Shock. Anger. Despair.

I reached out, brushing a lock of hair off her cheek before stroking my fingers down her soft skin to tip her chin back. "Don't be afraid to be curious about those things. Just because he made them sound dirty and terrifying doesn't mean they have to be."

"It's hard to… to think about it because on some level deep down…" She sobbed, throwing herself into my arms. I caught her and wrapped my arms around her as I had just a couple hours ago. This time, though, I urged her legs around my waist and carried her to the bedroom.

I sat on the edge of the bed, holding her, letting her cry. She trembled in my arms. Maybe from fear, but I thought it was mostly in arousal. I also knew it shamed her.

"I want some of the things they described," she whispered, her voice a mere whisper of sound. "But not with that man. Not with anyone but whom I choose."

"Nothin' wrong with that, baby girl. In fact, that's exactly the way it should be. You want to try somethin' new, you do it with someone you trust. Someone you want."

"It's not wrong? And I'd never want to do those things with just anyone."

"Not wrong at all. Everyone likes to experiment, but you get to choose who and what."

Calista pushed away from me slightly, looking into my face. "Are we really doing this whole old lady thing? You claiming me or whatever?"

I grinned. "You heard the options. Besides, I don't think you're as opposed to the thought as you try to pretend. I think you want to belong to me."

She huffed out a breath. "Maybe I want you to belong to me."

"I can work with that." I grinned. "Now. I want to kiss you. May I?"

Sucking in a breath, Calista nodded. "Yes, Ringo."

I grunted, sliding my hand around the back of her neck and pulling her down for a long, sweet kiss.

Chapter Eight

Calista

I was floating. Nothing existed in my world other than Ringo's lips pressed to mine. Until his tongue slipped into my mouth, tangling with mine in a slow dance of seduction, and I let out a needy whimper. His hands slid down my spine, gripping my ass gently, pulling me closer to him. The roughness of his beard brushed roughly against my skin, making me shiver in anticipation. His muscled body was so strong against me, and I melted into him as he deepened the kiss, running his hands up and down my back, leaving trails of fire wherever he touched.

Our tongues twined together, exploring each other's mouths, a journey in uncharted territory. At least it was for me. This was the closest I'd ever been to a man. It was the first time I'd ever felt this much lust and need. It was overwhelming and I was afraid it was eroding any good sense I might have had. I could taste whiskey from earlier on his tongue, mixed with the unique flavor of his kiss -- a blend of leather and motorcycle fumes that made my heart race even faster. He tasted like home and danger all at once -- an intoxicating combination that left me wanting more.

When we finally broke apart for air, our breathing was ragged and heavy. His blue eyes gleamed with desire as he looked at me intently. "You're fuckin' beautiful," he murmured hoarsely before claiming my lips again. This time, he nipped at them playfully before sucking on my bottom lip gently. My body responded instinctively, arching into him as I whimpered softly. "So fuckin' sexy."

I couldn't believe this was happening to me. Here I was with this ruggedly handsome man who seemed to know just how to touch me without scaring me too much but also keeping me on edge. My hands found their way up his chest, tracing the lines of ink adorning his skin just above his shirt while my fingers tangled in his hair.

My hands moved to his sides. I bunched the material of his shirt in my hands and tugged, needing to touch bare skin, to feel the warmth radiating from him. His muscles flexed under my touch, making me shiver with anticipation. Our mouths found each other again, his teeth scraping against my lower lip, leaving me breathless and wanting more. A low growl vibrated from him as he gripped my hips, pulling me closer to him. Heat grew between us and my face flushed.

Ringo leaned in to kiss me again, his tongue swirling around mine once more before he finally pulled away, panting slightly. "Fuck," he muttered with an appreciative grin on his face before leaning in to trail his lips down my neck. His beard tickled my skin as he kissed along my jawline, sending shivers down my spine. "You taste good." He sucked the delicate skin until I felt a slight sting. His mark. Judging by the satisfied grunt, he'd done it on purpose with that very intention.

His lips trailed lower, nipping gently at the sensitive skin above my breast while one hand slid underneath my T-shirt and trailed up my stomach to cup the same breast. I cried out softly at this new sensation, arching into him for more. My heart raced in response to his touch while his teeth scraped lightly against my skin, sending tingles through me.

"Ringo," I whispered breathlessly as he continued to nibble his way down the slope of my breast. "I think... I don't think I've ever wanted anyone like this before."

"That's a good thing," he murmured against my breast. "I'd hate to have to kill some bastard."

"Ringo!" I tried to push him away, but he just grunted and held me tighter. "You can't say stuff like that!"

"Why the fuck not? I'm a needy bastard. Don't want you thinkin' about anyone but me. Especially when we're makin' love."

God, that voice! He sounded so sexy I could actually feel my pussy gushing. Which turned me on even more. This man could melt the panties of any woman he set his sights on. And his attention was firmly on me. At least for now.

"I didn't think bikers could say that phrase."

He chuckled. "What? Makin' love?"

"Yeah. I thought it would be just fucking."

"I suppose it's fuckin' more often than makin' love, but make no mistake, Calista. The first time I take you, it'll be makin' love. I'm not a gentle man. Ain't got soft feelin's inside'a me." He gave me a wicked grin. "Sometimes, I'll use your body for my pleasure. Other times I'll give you everything you can take and not get myself off. But the first time's gonna be about us. Together. Gettin' to know each other."

I giggled nervously. "That sounds like fun."

"Oh, baby girl, it will definitely be fun." Yeah. I was in *way* the fuck over my head.

I couldn't even begin to think about sleeping with Ringo now. He was intoxicating, and I was terrified of what would happen if I gave in fully. But he smelled so damn good, like leather and sweat and his own unique scent that made me want to lean into him, to taste him even more. It might not be a good idea, but I wanted this with all my being. Wanted Ringo.

His beard tickled my neck as he nipped at it gently. The soft fabric of my shirt rubbed against my nipples where I was mashed against him, making me moan softly.

"You look so fucking hot when you blush." His voice was rough and low while his lips were tender on my skin. "I want to see you all flushed and needy, babe." He trailed lower, his tongue tracing the line of my collarbone before moving up the side of my neck once more. His lips found mine again, this time with a slow savor that threatened to undo me completely. His thumb feathered over one nipple where his hand was under my shirt. A small cry escaped me as it tightened in anticipation of his touch.

"I don't know if I'm ready for this," I whispered back, trying to keep my breathing steady as he kissed me again. "You're too much man for me, and I'm not too proud to admit it."

"You're wrong," he murmured against my lips, his teeth nibbling at them gently before he pulled away slightly. "You can take me on. You're stronger than you give yourself credit for. Don't worry about anything. I'll take care of you."

Ringo bent his knees, lifting me. Very carefully, he planted a knee and moved us to the center of the bed. His weight pressed me into the mattress, and I shivered in reaction.

"Never thought I'd like to be pinned down," I whispered.

Immediately, Ringo moved to put most of his weight on his arms. "Honey. Did I scare you?"

He sat back on his heels, pulling away but not leaving me. My legs were draped over his thighs, and he refused to let me close them.

"What?" I looked up at him, confused. Then I

started. "Did I say that out loud?"

He grinned down at me. "Yeah, baby girl. You did."

"What I meant was I never thought I'd like it. I don't like being restrained, but this is… different."

Ringo smiled, moving so that he could remove my boots but still had his hips wedged between my legs. Very slowly, Ringo lowered himself back on top of me fully. I whimpered but tightened my arms and legs around him to hold him close. I shivered, sweat erupting over my skin. My breath came in ragged gasps. And the guy had barely touched me!

"You OK, baby girl?"

All I could do was nod, my fingers tightening and releasing around his shirt. I was nervous and scared and excited and so fucking turned on! All at the same time.

"Nervous?"

I let out a small nervous laugh. "Yeah. A little."

Ringo smiled down at me, kissing my lips tenderly before responding. "Nervous is OK. Means you care about what's about to happen and I want you to care. I want you to expect I'll make this good for you. So lie back and let me pleasure you, baby girl. You don't have to think about anything other than telling me if you don't like something."

"You'll stop?" I hated the vulnerability in my voice, but this man was stripping me bare, figuratively. Soon he'd be doing it literally. I wasn't sure how I felt about it. I wanted him to show me more, to take me higher, but he'd expose my every flaw. I also wasn't sure I was strong enough to stop him, even if I was unsure of what he was doing.

"I will." He tilted his head looking at me intently. "Always." His gaze narrowed. "Don't think so hard, baby girl. Nothing happens you don't want or aren't ready for."

"How can you tell if I'm ready for something?"

"I'll know because I'm watching you. Paying attention to your reactions. You're scared but eager right now. I want you to embrace what we do together."

"You... you won't be mad if I need to stop?"

"Honey. No. Never. I'll stop and talk to you. You'll tell me what you didn't like, and I'll make it better or we'll try something different. The only wrong thing to do is to not speak up if you're uncomfortable. For any reason." He gave me a wicked grin that made my pussy quiver with need. "Then I'll find a way to make it better for you."

My heart pounded in my chest as Ringo's words sank in. I didn't want him to stop, but I was more than a little nervous. In a way, the nerves made me want him even more. It was a confusing mix of emotions and desires, but I trusted him. I nodded slowly, taking a deep breath to calm myself. "Okay," I whispered, my voice barely audible.

Ringo smiled reassuringly, his warm lips brushing against mine gently before trailing down my jawline again. He nipped at my earlobe, sending tingles down my spine, and then soothed it with gentle kisses. "You taste fucking delicious," he murmured against my skin. "Like sin and sweetness all rolled into one."

One hand traveled up my thigh to my hip and the waistband of my jeans. With a gentle tug, he undid the button, then the zip. He urged my hips up so he could slide the soft denim over my ass and down my legs. I wasn't wearing panties since I hadn't gone through what the women had brought me, so this was the moment.

Ringo looked down at me and his nostrils flared. A predator eying his prey. "So fuckin' gorgeous." His words sounded more for himself than for me. I drank them up, though. Like a man just emerging from the desert being handed a glass of ice water.

Ringo tugged his shirt off impatiently, never taking his gaze from my body. His hands rubbed slowly up my thighs before scraping down with a light abrasion to my knees.

Unable to help myself, I arched my back, crying out. His gaze was firmly on my pussy. I felt a trickle of moisture leaking out and Ringo's gaze got heavy-lidded, and a satisfied smile parted his lips.

"Oh, yeah, baby girl. So responsive. You like that, don't you?"

"Ringo…" I gasped out his name on a surprised breath.

Slowly, he lay back on top of me, his belly over my mound. I canted my hips, needing friction between my legs. He threaded his fingers through my hair and kissed me again, letting his tongue slide inside my mouth with lazy strokes.

I melted under his kiss, but little zings of pleasure also made me tense convulsively. It was almost too much. Overstimulation in the extreme.

"That's it, my precious girl. You need to come. Don't you." It wasn't a question.

"What is this?" My plea was almost wild. I'd never known something like this possible. There was something wild inside me, clawing to get out. It was that painful.

"Don't fight it. Just let it happen." Ringo sounded strained and beads of sweat dotted his forehead, but I couldn't focus on anything but the need blooming out of control inside me.

With a growl, Ringo shifted his body and thrust his hips against me. I was naked from the waist down. Ringo was shirtless, but still had on his jeans. The new position was exactly what I needed. With a scream -- with several screams actually -- wave after wave of pleasure so intense it bordered on pain crashed over me. My muscles spasmed. My vision tunneled...

And all I could see was Ringo.

Chapter Nine

Ringo

That was it. I was gonna come in my fucking pants. Never had I witnessed anything like what Calista was experiencing now. She was completely lost in pleasure, a look of utter euphoria on her face. And she was the most beautiful creature I'd ever fuckin' seen.

I kissed her softly, trying to bring her down carefully before driving her back up again. If I had my way, once she'd rested, Calista would be like this for days. I wanted to explore every single fantasy she had and help her make some more. I wanted to be the man to show her the joys of sex, and I wanted her to always associate sex and pleasure with me. No one else. Not even as a passing memory she hadn't thought about in years. I wanted her to know her needs and desires were important and valid and never wrong or dirty.

"That's it, baby girl. That's it. You came so beautifully for me, didn't you?"

"Ringo." Her voice was a whisper of wonder. Her eyes wide. Sweat coated her skin in a shimmery sheen in the morning light filtering through the window.

I smiled down at her. "You back with me?"

She smiled a slow, lazy smile. A woman well-satisfied. "I never left you. It was all you."

"No, honey. It was all you. Much as I'd love to take the credit for it, you're the most naturally sensual creature I've ever seen."

"I've never felt anything like that. I thought things like that were only in books."

"Oh, it's real. And I'm gonna help you explore every single one of them."

"Yes." She nodded her head eagerly. "More!"

I laughed, hugging her close. "Soon, baby girl. You need some sleep and so do I. We've both been up all night, but I'm bettin' you didn't exactly sleep in yesterday. Did you?"

"No." She shivered and shook her head. "My stepfather liked to keep a schedule. So, no matter what, everyone had to be up at six in the morning, every morning."

I've never wanted to kill anyone more in my life. And, God knew, I'd killed more than my share. As enforcer of the club, that was one of my jobs. If someone needed killing. This guy, Borris Illivitch, not only needed to die, he needed to *fucking* die.

"Well, good thing you don't have to do what he says now, ain't it?"

She smiled up at me. "No. I don't, do I?"

"Nope. In fact, I'm gonna have to insist that you do exactly whatever the fuck you wanna do from now on."

The second I said it, I knew it was the exact wrong thing to say if I wanted her to get some rest. Calista got a wicked gleam in her eye, and I knew I was fucked.

"Oh, really." She pushed me over to my back, throwing her leg over my hips to straddle me. She braced her hands on my chest while she shimmied her hips over my jeans-covered dick. "Well, I want to do this."

"I'm so fucked," I muttered, gritting my teeth even as I gripped her hips, helping her move. She paused in her movements. I could tell she really wanted to ride me, to take control of her own pleasure but was unsure how to go about doing it. She wasn't a teenager, but, if Illivitch had wanted to preserve her virginity to get a good price for her, then it was entirely possible he'd made it so she couldn't pleasure herself. Maybe she'd just never felt the need before. Whatever the reason, I knew in my heart, everything I'd done with Calista to this point had been her first. She might not be innocent in mind, but her body was dealing with things she'd never felt before and it was overwhelming her. Overwhelming could be a good thing, if she surrendered to it and just let me have her. If she fought it, those feelings might scare her. Until she got used to them. I intended to help her get used to them. I intended to help her a lot.

She rocked over me, her body shuddering occasionally when the sensations grew too intense. She didn't back down, though. Right before my eyes, I watched this brave beauty embrace her pleasure, boldly seeking it out even though she was unsure of herself.

She still had on her T-shirt, but I wanted her naked. I wanted to ride her hard, make her scream my name as she came. I was trying with everything I had to be the good guy here, but she was deliberately chiseling away my control. Her first time should be soft words and delicate touches, but I wasn't sure I could manage that just now.

"Ringo? Please help me." Her plea was soft and needy even as her body was aggressive atop me. Her hips snapped over and over as she rubbed over me. I knew what she needed. But I wasn't making that move. If she did it herself, I wouldn't stop her, but I absolutely would not push this girl any further than she was willing to push herself.

"Take what you need or tell me what you want."

"I want..." She shuddered again, as if the very thought of voicing her needs turned her on. "I want you to fuck me."

"This mornin's about your pleasure, baby girl. You want me inside you, you're gonna have to do it yourself. Ain't takin' advantage of you like this."

She narrowed her gaze at me. "Take advantage of me like... what?"

"You're scared. There's a threat hanging over you. You just met your dad, who I'm guessing you only half expected to welcome you. I'm guessin' you're feelin' pretty vulnerable and overwhelmed."

She shrugged. "Maybe. What's that got to do with anything?"

"I don't want you doin' something you might regret later. Ain't too proud to admit I wouldn't stop you if you wanted to put my dick inside you, but I ain't gonna be the one to put it there."

"You think I won't?" Calista was angry. And just like that, every ounce of blood in my body went straight to my cock. "Because I will totally pull out your dick, *hawk tuah* that thang, and take my virginity with it."

There was a beat of silence while I processed what she'd just said. "*Hawk tuah?*" I chuckled. "I thought you were some sheltered little thing. How the fuck do you know what that means?"

"I had my ways of smuggling in contraband. Lifted more than one phone off my stepfather's friends. Once the phone's unlocked, I take it and turn off the security so I can get in when I want." She shrugged. "Men like that don't like any inconvenience, like biometrics or PINs. They also think they're too powerful for anyone to take anything from them, to say nothing of losing it. More than half of the phones I lifted had all the security features turned off. YouTube is my friend." The smug look on her face melted any resistance I thought I possessed against fucking this girl today. It was happening. Likely sooner rather than later.

"Little witch. What would have happened if you'd gotten caught?"

"Didn't care. The reward was worth the risk to me."

"I'm gonna have my hands full with you, aren't I?"

"I certainly hope so. If you don't, I'm not doing my job."

Then she reached for the button of my jeans and flicked it open with her fingers. When she slid the zip down, the relief was almost immediate. I couldn't stop the sharp grunt as her fingers brushed my cock through my boxers. Instead of pulling back like I expected she might, afraid she'd hurt me or something, she gave me a satisfied grin. Right as she pulled at my waistband and pulled my cock free.

"Yep," I groaned in a strained voice. "Handful."

"I'd say you were more than a handful, but what do I know?"

"Quite a lot, apparently."

Calista stroked me. Up and down. I watched in fascination as she tucked her hand against her pussy entrance, swiping her fingers through her own moisture. Then she stroked my cock, wetting me.

With excruciating slowness, Calista sank down on to my cock. I saw her wince as I took her virginity, saw the streak of blood when she rose back up just before she sank down again. I should have been ensuring she wasn't hurting, but she kept moving and I was beyond thinking.

After the third time she rose and fell on me, I gripped her hips, taking control because I simply to

God couldn't stop myself any longer. Again, Calista surprised me by getting this relieved look that immediately morphed into complete euphoria.

Her eyes slid closed as I fucked up into her, making her bounce with every thrust. I could see her tits bouncing under the shirt she still wore. That wouldn't do at all.

"Take off your shirt, Calista." I kept my hold on her hips, never missing a stroke. Seconds later, she'd whipped off her shirt and was... cupping her tits?

"Ah, fuckin' hell," I groaned. I wanted to roll us over so I was on top of her, pinning her like before. I didn't because I loved looking up at her like this. The look of wonder and excitement on her face while my body worked hers was not something I wanted to miss. I wanted the full view, to see every blush and shiver over her skin.

"Ringo!" She threw back her head and screamed. Her long hair spilled down her back, tickling my balls, and that was it. I was fucking done, because this woman was taking everything I had to give and embracing it. Just like I wanted her to.

I roared my release, bellowing as loud as she screamed. If I didn't want her to hold back, I wasn't holding myself back from her either.

Calista fell on top of me, her breath ragged. Her hair wove us together where it clung to my beard and her sweat-dampened skin. She was limp as a sleepy kitten, draped over me contentedly. "I can't move."

I was still inside her, my cock twitching occasionally. Usually right after her pussy contracted around me, milking me of every last fucking drop. "No one said you had to." I kissed the top of her head, nuzzling her in an effort to bring her comfort and to assure myself this was actually real. What I'd just experienced with Calista, a little slip of an inexperienced young woman, was nothing short of mind-altering. I knew this was my woman. The woman I was always meant to be with.

"I'm sure you'd be more comfortable without someone lying on top of you." She still didn't move. I had to smile.

"Nope. Perfectly fine the way I am."

"Um, Ringo?" She was still boneless and didn't stiffen, but I heard the slight strain in her voice. Like she was uncertain with herself or afraid. I didn't like the thoughts of either.

"What is it, baby girl?"

"We, uh…" She cleared her throat. "That is, you came inside me. We didn't use a condom."

It took a second for what she'd said to penetrate my brain and I waited. For several seconds. Then a couple more.

Any second now…

There was no panic. No dread. What there was, was extreme and total satisfaction. Like I knew for absolute certainty I'd just gotten her pregnant when nothing could have been further from the truth. But it felt like I was right. I found the thought of Calista's belly growing round with my baby more arousing than it should have been. Maybe.

My cock shot hard almost the second the realization hit me. Calista stiffened and pushed off my chest far enough to look at me. Her eyes widened and her lips parted in a silent "O" of surprise. Then she grinned.

"You like the thought you might've knocked me up? Do you even know my father? Because, no matter if he basically gave you to me or not, if you get me pregnant this quick, you know he's gonna kill you.

Right?"

I couldn't help but laugh at her horrified expression before pulling her back to me for a kiss. I rolled us over, rocking my hips from side to side as I kept myself seated deep inside her.

"Yeah, babe. Known him a helluva long time longer than you. And I can tell you with great confidence that your assessment of the situation is entirely one hundred percent correct."

As I'd hoped, Calista burst into giggles. I nuzzled my way to her neck, threatening to take a bite out of her. She squealed in delight but didn't fight me at all. It was like she soaked up the positive attention and touches in any form. Borris Illivitch had a lot to answer for. You know. Before I let him die.

I gradually changed my touches from tickling and playful to more coaxing and caressing. She sighed and found my mouth with hers in a sweet kiss.

I rocked into her, one slow, lazy thrust after another. "You're beautiful, baby girl. So Goddamned beautiful."

Her pussy clamped around my cock as I continued to stroke in and out of her. She met every one with a rise of her hips.

I'd told her I wanted to make love to her, but I honestly wasn't sure I understood exactly what that meant. I knew I wanted her to feel cherished and wanted. Loved. Those weren't things I knew how to express or even what they felt like. Until this moment.

"I'm yours, Ringo. All yours. Just remember you're all mine too."

"I swear to you, Calista. For as long as I live, I'll be yours. We'll work together to make this work between us. Yes?"

The smile she gave me was nothing short of

glorious. "Yes."

The next time she came -- and took me with her -- I settled her in front of me, my arm around her waist, and held her tight. This was where Calista belonged. If I had my way, this was where she'd always stay.

Chapter Ten

Calista

The next week represented the happiest I'd been since before my mother died. Ringo and I barely left the little house the first two days. It wasn't until Dom came pounding on the front door with a scowl and threats of unmanning Ringo if he didn't bring me out to be with him and the rest of the Grim Road.

Not only had I gotten to know Ringo better, but I'd started forming a bond with Dom. He told me stories about my mother. When he did, he'd get this distant, soft look on his face. Her memory was obviously something he cherished. It made me feel better about running to him. He loved my mother. It was easy to tell. He was trying to love me the same as I was trying to love him.

"Ringo!" Dom bellowed from across the yard as he marched toward the house. I was sitting on the porch with Ringo, holding hands and talking. The man loved to touch me. In fact, the second I moved to go greet my father, Ringo growled and pulled me into his lap.

"Mine," he growled up at Dom. "Go away."

Dom gave him an impatient look. "She might be yours, but she was mine first."

"Was not." Ringo lifted his chin stubbornly. "I'd argue she was mine long before she was yours."

"What? A whole minute and a half? She came here for me."

"And she found me."

"I'm not a bone for you two junkyard dogs to fight over." I tried to sound put out, but I snuggled into Ringo, soaking up the attention. I loved his touch. I hadn't had much positive affection since my mother died.

"Of course, you're not," Dom said hastily. He knelt in front of us, taking my hand in both of his before kissing my fingers. "You're my daughter and this lout is taking up all your time."

"I've got all the time you want, Dad." I smiled up at him. "I'll always have time for you."

The smile he gave me was genuine and happy. He reached for me, and I would have happily gone to him for the big bear hug he always gave me, but Ringo tightened his hold.

"Mine."

Dom rolled his eyes. "Let an old man have some time with his only daughter."

"Old man?" Ringo snorted. "I'll remember that."

"Give me. My daughter." Dom's voice was stern, but he winked at me. I got the feeling he and Ringo loved bickering back and forth. They were definitely close friends. From what I could tell, they worked closely together. What one knew, the other did. What enemy one fought, so did the other.

"Go fuck yourself." Ringo's hold tightened on me, and he bared his teeth at Dom.

"Christ, Ringo." Dom scowled. "I want my daughter."

"Jesus, old man," Ringo grumbled. "Fine. Whine a little more, why don't you?"

"Pretty sure it's you who's whinin'." Dom stood, reaching for me. When I got to my feet, he gave me the big, tight hug I'd come to crave from the older man. "It's good to see you, honey."

I signed contentedly. "It's good to see you too."

"You two are comin' to the picnic, right?"

"No," Ringo said at the same time I said, "Yes."

"When did you turn into such a party pooper,

Ringo?" Dom chuckled, obviously enjoying the banter. I'd never admit it to Ringo, but I was loving it too. It felt good to be fussed over by people who had my well-being at heart.

"Since you came over and tried to take my girl." Ringo stood and pulled me back into his arms. "Gimme."

I couldn't help myself. I laughed as I wrapped my arms around Ringo, burying my face in his chest. "You two are horrible. But I love you both." The confession slipped out before I realized it. When both men stilled, I stiffened in Ringo's arms.

"Oh, no, baby girl," Ringo said, tightening his grip on me. "No takesie backsies."

That really got a laugh out of me. "Honestly, where do you come up with this shit?"

I heard Dom snort. "You *have* met Lemon. Right?"

"Point taken." I turned in Ringo's arms. He grunted but didn't try to stop me. "And yes. We're going to the picnic."

"Good. If Lemon had to come after you, she said she was moving you in with her and Rocket so she could get to know her new sister."

I gave a happy sigh. "God, I love it here."

Both men smiled. "Good. This is your home now." Dom winked at me. "Come on then. Let's get to the clubhouse before Lemon goes on a rampage."

Laughing, we all made our way toward the clubhouse, a sturdy building set back from the main house, surrounded by giant, leafy trees. The path was littered with fallen leaves that crunched satisfyingly under our feet. The afternoon sun cast long shadows that danced on the ground as we walked.

As we approached, the sounds of laughter and

music floated toward us, promising a lively gathering. Lemon was at the heart of the picnic, her laughter infectious, drawing people to her like moths to a flame.

"Ah, there they are!" Lemon exclaimed as we entered the clearing. She bounded over to us with Rocket not far behind. She pulled me into a tight embrace. "Everything good?" She whispered her question right at my ear, and I knew she was making sure I was still good to be with Ringo.

"It is. Ringo is wonderful. Dom is the best dad ever. I'd have hated him as a child 'cause I'd never have gotten away with anything." I pulled back, grinning like a loon. "I love it. I love them both so much." I didn't even try not to smile. "Thank you for everything. I know you've been the one making sure we have everything we need so we can have some time alone."

"Pfft." She waved a hand in the air. "That was for you. Ringo can damned well fend for himself. He's a big boy."

"That he is," I muttered. When Lemon barked out a laugh, I realized I'd said that last part out loud and exactly how it sounded. I had a moment where I thought I'd be embarrassed, but all that bubbled up was laughter. I grinned. "Well? He is!"

Lemon hugged me again before taking my hand. "Come on. Me and the other old ladies saved you a seat."

I looked over my shoulder at Ringo who was gazing at me with affection and pride. He nodded his head, and I smiled back at him. Then I let Lemon take me to the other women.

"Ain't no club girls allowed today," Lemon said, "but it won't always be that way. Stake your claim early so they know you mean business."

"But Ringo said the vest would do that. I'm not to leave the house without wearing it."

"True. And it will help." She tapped her chin. "But women are a catty lot." Then she grinned again. "Besides, the fun is in the shock value. I recommend stomping through the middle of them wearing the blood of your enemies. Works like a charm."

I chuckled again, but a tall woman who looked like a pink paint factory exploded on her smiled down at the smaller woman with affection. "She's not joking. I fought by her side last time." The woman had a slight Russian accent. She was dressed in pink leather and pink boots. I was told her bike was also pink. In fact, I'd seen her and Lemon both riding pink Harleys. This woman -- her name was Venus -- was on a whole other level, though. She had long, pink hair, pink nails that looked sharp as daggers, and pink *eyes*. Who the fuck had pink eyes? I'd heard of Venus but hadn't met her yet. I liked her immediately. "Stand up to club girls and they will respect boundaries you set." She smiled, reaching out a hand to me which I took. Her grip was firm, but not so strong it hurt. Yes. This woman would be a friend.

"Thanks for the advice. I'll keep it in mind for future conflict."

Venus lifted her chin, a proud smile on her face. She was older than the rest of the women at the table, but wasn't wearing a property vest. She acted like a proud mother gathering her children around the table. Which was not something I was going to point out. To anyone. I got the feeling it would be the height of bad form and that, while everyone else might get a kick out of the other woman being labeled a mother figure, Venus likely wouldn't appreciate it.

"Come sit." Olivia, Bear's woman, held out her

hand to me. There was a spot between her and Evelyn they'd saved for me. "We've got stuff to plan and world domination to contemplate."

Cecilia brought a girl of about eight or so to the table with her. With the girl's dark locks and pale skin, she could be the woman's daughter, but she wasn't. She stayed with either Lemon and Rocket, or Gina. Gina was shy, but Lemon and the other women were helping her. I also thought Falcon might have a thing for her. He hovered over the woman. Constantly. Even if he was in the background like he was now. Gina gave me a shy smile, lowering her gaze like she thought I'd reject her.

"It's good to see you again, Gina." I always made a point to speak to her. Though she constantly had one of the women with her -- likely watching out for her -- she seemed so beat down and scared all the time. At first it concerned me. If she didn't feel safe, was I? But I'd soon learned it was because she'd had an uncertain and rough start when she first came here. I didn't know the full story but all the men in the club were unfailingly polite and gentle with her. Over the week I'd been here, I'd witnessed how careful everyone was with her. It was just one more thing that made me realize what a good choice I'd made in following my mother's instructions and coming here the first opportunity I got.

As always, she got a surprised look on her face. This time, however, she smiled afterward. "It's good to see you, too, Calista. Are you settling in?"

"I am. Though, I worry there's not enough of me to go around. I'm still getting used to being with Ringo but I need to get to know my... uh, that is, Dom." I wasn't ashamed to call him my dad, but I wasn't sure he wanted me referring to him that way around the rest of the club. I was still trying to wade through everything, but so far, any fears I had about these people not accepting me had been completely unfounded.

"My *daughter* has been feelin' her way through." Dom gave me a chastising look. Yeah. I got it. Since the first time I'd called him dad, he'd corrected me every time I'd used his name. I should have known, but I was still unsure. "Thank you for helping make her feel welcome, Gina." Dom gave the other woman a warm, kind smile which Gina returned.

"She's very sweet." Her gaze darted to mine. "I hope we can be friends."

"We are already," I said hastily. "Everyone's been so nice. I appreciate you guys taking me in. I hope we can do some things together soon, Gina."

"I know of some real fun we can have." Dom grinned at me.

My eyes got wide, and I shook my head. "Oh now. Last time you said that you had me out in the woods for survival training. It's fucking *hot*."

He lifted his chin, an expression of hurt on his face even as his eyes danced in merriment. He loved teasing me and I loved giving him shit. "Taught you how to start a fire with damp wood, didn't I?"

"Yes. I also lost about a gallon of water in the form of sweat. Thanks, Dad. But no thanks."

Dom grumbled, but it got Gina to giggle. Dom grinned at me and winked at Gina before wandering off. Ringo grinned and nodded, indicating I should spend time with the women. He backed off, but much like Falcon, he hovered off in the distance. I noticed the men of the other women doing the same thing. In fact, it felt like they'd formed a loose circle around us. Like a circle of protection.

"Shouldn't we invite the other women?" I gave Lemon a questioning look.

She shrugged. "We could. But, since this is your first gathering with all of us, I thought it might be better if we saved that for another time. You know. After you come in soaked in the blood of your enemies like I told you."

I blinked. "Oh. You *were* serious." I glanced at Venus who just shrugged and grinned. Gina ducked her head, but I could see her smile. "Well. Shit." That got her to chuckle a little.

Lemon chuckled along, her laughter ringing clear and bold, a stark contrast to Gina's more subdued mirth. "It's a rite of passage around here," she said teasingly, clinking her glass against mine. "But don't worry, we'll ease you into it. No bloodshed required in your first week."

The menu consisted of burgers, dogs, and pulled pork. There was potato salad, baked beans, and, of course, deviled eggs. Because what was a cookout without deviled eggs and pulled pork BBQ? I made a pig out of myself (no pun intended) and ate some of everything. Dessert consisted of some kind of s'mores treat cooked on the grill. Looked like a hollowed-out marshmallow with chocolate chip cookie dough in the middle, then put on the grill until the marshmallows were brown and crispy. Chocolate was drizzled over it and served with graham crackers. And it was *delicious*!

I was just finishing my last bite when there was a commotion coming from the back of the property. Two men on motorcycles circled around the main gathering and rode straight to Rocket. Lemon's gaze was fixed on the trio as she continued the conversation going on around us.

I glanced up at Ringo. His posture suggested

something was wrong. He stood there, his hand on the sidearm at his hip. Not everyone went around the compound armed, but Ringo was the club enforcer. He and Dom were always armed.

"I'll be back," Lemon said, wiping her mouth and standing.

The women all made eye contact with their men much like I did with Ringo and Dom. I didn't miss how the circle of protection tightened around us as the men moved closer.

"What's happening?" My gaze moved to the other women, all of whom looked equally puzzled as me.

"Not sure." Evelyn found Knox's gaze. The other man nodded to her, then gave a shrill whistle. Immediately, all the kids and younger adults in the area ran to the table.

Anesya, Evelyn's daughter, was the first there, followed closely by Euphemia. The girls were close to the same age and were fast friends. I never saw one without the other. Luke, Anesya's brother, was next. He responded more slowly and was looking around him as he made sure Anesya and Effie got to the table with the women. The second they were, he veered off and went to Knox.

A few seconds later, several men who hadn't been outside rushed from the clubhouse, all of them checking sidearms and rifles before climbing on their bikes and heading toward the back of the property, Ringo in the lead.

Dom hurried straight to me. "We'll be back soon, sweetheart. You stay with Apple."

"What is it?"

"Nothin' for you to worry about, honey. Just go with Apple and the old ladies. Stay with them until me and Ringo come for you."

He would have gone back to the other men, but I put a hand on his arm, halting him. "Tell me. Is it Borris?"

Dom sighed. "Yeah, baby. They've not found us, but they're too close for comfort. We'll take care of this. Don't worry." He leaned in and kissed the top of my head before shrugging off my hold and going back to the other men.

"I don't like this," Olivia muttered. "Something's not right."

I watched as Lemon and Rocket had a heated discussion. I didn't miss that it was only after the other men were gone. Until that point, they'd stood shoulder to shoulder, backing each other up on whatever was going on.

"Yeah," I said. "Same."

Apple stood then, seeming to know her role in all this. She'd waited until Lemon nodded in her direction and went with Rocket before she took charge. "Let's go," she said. "Safe house and into the panic room."

I probably should have been scared that they needed a panic room, but one thing I'd learned since I'd been here was that these guys meant business. They were off the grid for a reason, but they never took safety lightly.

We followed Apple. As we headed to the safe house -- which was in the very center of what they called the family area -- several more women and some older children met us, following without complaint. I didn't know everyone yet, but I did know that there was more than one club girl in our midst, so I figured this represented all the women in the compound. Well, except for Venus. She and Lemon had gone with the men to what I could only assume was to take care of the problem. I wasn't even going to pretend to myself that people weren't about to die. If they were Borris's people, I wasn't all that broken up about it. I did feel like a coward for not going with Ringo. Not that I'd had much choice in the matter.

"Come on." Apple looped her arm through mine. I hadn't realized I'd been slowing until she did. "We're all supposed to go here and stay until Rocket and Lemon come for us."

"I want to go with them."

"Me too," she said with a grin. "Unfortunately, the only women Rocket allows at stuff like this are Lemon and Venus. Venus because that woman can be fuckin' scary sometimes. Lemon because Rocket would like to keep his balls. When Lemon wants something, she gets it. One way or another." Apple smiled at me, but there was strain on her face. She wasn't happy about not being included either.

We moved with a hasty but controlled pace toward the safe house. The air around us felt thick, charged with the tension and unspoken fears of what lay ahead. The kids and the other old ladies were filing inside the house along with the remaining women -- I had trouble calling them club whores or even club girls. I got there was a whole other culture I hadn't gotten used to yet, but I couldn't wrap my mind around it yet. Apple and Cecilia tried to hurry me inside, but something felt just that little bit... off.

"Come on, Calista." Apple took my hand, tugging me after her. "In you go."

I nodded and was about to let them force the issue when someone moved from the side of the house in our direction. Apple must have sensed something too because she turned her head in the same direction, frowning.

"Redwood? Aren't you helping the rest of the guys?"

"Yep." He pulled a gun from behind his back and let it hang at his side. "Helpin' bring this wayward child home to her daddy."

I gasped. Apple pursed her lips. I could see her tongue curling behind her lips, and she let out a very loud, very shrill whistle.

Two things happened at once. Redwood raised his gun, pulling the trigger. And Apple dove, shoving me aside...

And jerked as the bullet struck her before she collapsed to the ground.

Chapter Eleven

Ringo

The second I shut off my bike, I heard the sharp whistle, faint with distance. Had I been three seconds later, I'd have missed it. My head snapped in the direction of the noise. Then there was a gunshot. A scream. Then nothing.

"Rocket!"

"Go, Ringo!" Dom sounded as panicked as I felt. "Get to my daughter!"

I knew Dom would order others to go with me, but I wasn't waiting. If Calista hadn't gotten to the safe room, if some bastard had shot her...

I'd been through hell before I came to Grim Road. I'd tortured, been tortured. I'd fought for my life and the lives of my team. I'd lived with monsters only to kill them when they least expected it. Never once had I truly felt fear. Not like I felt now.

I was on my bike, full throttle. Straight back to Calista. My woman.

Soon after, I spotted Redwood and two women on the ground in front of the house. As I got closer, I realized it was Apple and Calista. I couldn't tell which one of them was hurt, but I didn't miss the gun in Redwood's hand. Especially when he raised it to point at the women on the ground.

"Redwood!"

I was afraid he might shoot the women, but he turned and fired at me twice. I felt the wind from the first bullet whiz past my face. The second one kissed my cheek with a fiery tongue.

I grunted, jerking and nearly laying the bike down as I sped toward them. I heard Calista scream as Redwood turned back to the women. There was movement in front of Redwood. Calista and Apple struggled with something, then Calista launched herself at Redwood.

"Calista!" It only took seconds to reach her, but it felt like an eternity. It was like everything was happening in slow motion and I was slogging through quicksand.

I was almost there, tensing to spring and tackle the son of bitch to the ground when Redwood fell. Calista was on top of him with what looked like a chef's knife. She screamed like a fucking banshee, driving the knife into his chest over and over. Apple crawled away from Calista and Redwood, but not to get to safety. She saw the gun and made a grab for it, rolling toward me.

"Take that motherfucker out, Ringo!" Her demand was growled through clenched teeth.

I snagged the gun from her. "Calista! Roll!"

I must have put enough command in my voice to penetrate because Calista didn't hesitate to do what I said. The second she was away, I skidded to my knees beside Redwood, the barrel of my gun against his forehead. Calista's knife was still sticking out of his chest and the man was bleeding like a stuck pig. Blood bubbled from his lips and nose with every breath.

"You fuckin' piece of fuckin' shit," I snarled at the man. "You were my brother."

Redwood snorted, spraying blood over my face. I spat back at him, digging the gun into his skin harder. He just gave me an evil smile. "I'm not the only one, Ringo. Dom and Rocket... are crazy to think... you've not got... enemies... here..." He was struggling with each word, and I knew he wouldn't last long.

I pulled the knife from his chest slowly, taking great pleasure with every wince from the fucker. I put it to his throat. "Tell me who else, Redwood."

He laughed. "Go fuck yourself, Ringo."

"You first." Very slowly and deliberately, I cut his throat. When the blood started flowing from one side of his neck as I severed his external jugular, Redwood whimpered, clamping his hand to the blood pouring from the vein. I kept going, inch by slow inch.

"Ringo?" He gasped, a look of surprise on his face. I paused, raising my eyebrow. When he sucked in a breath but said nothing else, I shrugged. Then continued cutting, slicing through his trachea to the other external jugular vein. He gurgled a couple more times, gripping my vest with his bloody hand. Blood flowed freely into the grass and gravel, staining our home with the blood of our own.

I stood, tossing the knife to the ground as I turned to find Calista. She was huddled beside Apple, her shirt off and bunched in her hand where she pressed it to Apple's chest.

For her part, Apple appeared calm, but in pain. No doubt every single breath hurt. She met my gaze. "Will you get Lemon for me, please, Ringo?"

I nodded, pulling out my phone and calling Rocket. He answered on the first ring.

"What happened?"

"Redwood's dead. Apple's been shot. Don't know how bad, but we need Bullet."

There was a murmur of voices, then Rocket was back. "He's on the way. Lemon too."

"Good. She asked for her sister. Did you find anything on your end?"

"Dom found evidence someone was on the west side just beyond the boundary. That's what triggered Crush's proximity alert. Whoever it was is long gone."

"Probably because he was alerted we were on to

him."

"What?" The president's voice was suddenly sharp and angry. Even more so than he was when we first took off after an intruder into our territory.

"Redwood shot Apple. Calista stabbed Redwood. I cut his fuckin' throat. He said he wasn't the only one. Not the only enemy we have here."

"You believe him?"

"Above my pay grade. My gut says he's lying, but I'm not willing to take that chance."

"Byte and Crush have it. They'll get to the bottom of this, and they'll get to the bottom of it soon." The barely controlled rage in Rocket's voice was very clear. I wasn't sure I'd ever heard my president this angry. There was a pause, and I knew what was coming next. "Why'd you kill Redwood?"

"You mean besides because he shot Apple and had turned back to either finish her off or shoot Calista?"

"Yeah, Ringo," Rocket snapped. "Other than that."

"He was dead anyway. Calista didn't fuck around with him. Stabbed him at least five or six times with a fucking big-ass sharp knife. He was dying anyway. I didn't want her to be the one to kill him."

Rocket was silent and I could almost see him scrubbing a hand over his face. "Yeah. Sorry, brother."

As I finished the call with Rocket, a big-ass SUV skidded to a halt in front of the house. Bullet jumped out of the passenger's side while Leather and Falcon exited the driver's side. Leather driving, Falcon in the back seat with a long backboard.

Bullet took a quick look at Apple before putting her on the narrow board Falcon laid beside her.

"Get her to the truck. I need to look Calista

over."

"I'm fine. Not a scratch," Calista assured him. "I promise."

"Not even a tiny scratch?" Bullet gave her a stern look.

"No. I swear."

Bullet gave me a hard look. "You make sure."

"Don't worry. Take care of Apple. If I need you, I'll bring Calista to your clinic."

"I'll let you know if I need to get her to a hospital."

"What do you mean if?" Calista got to her feet, even though I tried to keep her on the ground. "There is no *if*! She's been fucking *shot*!"

Bullet gave her a tight smile. I knew the other man wanted to get Apple to his clinic so he could properly assess the damage, but he also took time to reassure my woman her friend would be seen to properly.

"I swear to you, Calista. I won't take a chance with Apple's life. Besides the fact Lemon would kill me, I'd never deny anyone care who needed it. Especially one of our women."

"How would you explain this?" I knew Bullet would have trouble with an extensive gunshot wound if he had to take her to the hospital. Even if he took her to his old hospital where he could still get things done off the books, stuff like that was required to be reported.

He shrugged. "We'll figure that out if it comes to it. But I truly think Apple will be fine here. I don't think it's as bad as it looks."

That seemed to put Calista at ease because she let me pick her up to carry her inside the house. Before I took her inside, though, I wanted her to see that Apple wouldn't be alone. I saw Lemon approach as Falcon and Leather carried Apple on the board to the SUV and loaded her into the back.

Lemon got there right before they got her inside the truck and hurried in that direction. She stopped briefly to punt Redwood in the head with her booted foot before climbing in with her sister.

"I need to go with Apple," Calista said shakily. "I don't want her to be alone if Lemon needs to leave."

"We'll go in a minute. Just let me look you over first. Besides, do you honestly think Lemon is going to leave her sister?"

"No," she said. Calista buried her face in my chest and cried. "This is my fault." Her voice was muffled, but I heard her clearly.

"Hey. No," I said firmly, sitting on the couch in the living room. Thankfully, everyone else was in the panic room, and I could take a few moments with Calista to calm her fears and maybe look her over quickly. "This isn't your fault."

"I brought these people straight to your door! I don't know how they found me, but none of this would have happened if I hadn't come here! Redwood said he was taking me back to Borris."

"You did what you had to do to survive. Redwood was already here. If this hadn't flushed him out, something else would have. None of this is on you." I gripped her chin and turned her face up to mine. "You get me? That motherfucker Illivitch's gonna fuckin' die, though."

She nodded. "Yes. Please." Then she wrapped her arms around my neck and cried silently against my skin.

I only hoped Dom didn't find Illivitch before I did. This was one kill I desperately wanted.

Chapter Twelve

Calista

The ride to Bullet's clinic was a blur. Ringo took me in an old pickup because he thought I was too shaky to ride behind him on his bike. He wasn't wrong. The thought that I might not see my friend again living and breathing and laughing and giving everyone shit clawed at me.

"She'll be OK, you know." Ringo squeezed my hand as he pulled the truck outside what I could only assume was Bullet's place. "Bullet wouldn't take a chance with her life. If she needs more care than she can get here, he'll make sure she has the best. She's strong."

"I shouldn't have called him Peckerwood," I muttered, inanely. "Then maybe he wouldn't have done this." It was a stupid thing to say, but it was the only thought ringing in my head. No matter what Ringo said, this felt like my fault. On multiple counts. "I forced my way in here, I insulted a member of your club. If Apple dies --"

"Stop!" Ringo barked out the command, then pulled me onto his lap to straddle him. I went back to burying my face in his neck because it was comforting. And because I didn't want to face the recrimination in his eyes. I should have realized at this point that Ringo wouldn't let me get away with hiding from him. He gently forced my face up, so I had to look at him. "You did exactly what you were supposed to do. Dom gave your mom the information to get you here and you used it. If anyone is to blame for that, it's Dom. What you don't seem to get is that Dom did exactly what he was supposed to do, too. If that means bringing danger to our door, you're most certainly worth it. To Dom. To me. Apple, too. I guarantee you, *no one* blames anyone but Illivitch and Redwood. Certainly not you."

I shook my head hard. "You don't know that."

He gripped my shoulders, giving me a little shake back. "I do. I absolutely do. This is my club. I've known most of these men my whole adult life. Since I was in the service. Certainly after coming here."

"But Redwood --"

"Was a rat bastard. Look." He scrubbed a hand over his face. "I'm going to tell you something. Should have before, but we've been getting to know each other. I had no desire to interrupt bonding with you. I wanted you solidly in my corner before we went into why this club is even here."

"I don't understand."

He gave me a gentle smile as he wiped tears from under my eyes with his thumbs. "We're not good guys, Calista. We have our own moral codes. Not everyone is the same. Some of us are OK with doing shit others aren't. But we've all done shit that could land us in prison or shot."

I narrowed my gaze at him. "What are you trying to tell me?"

"Every single person in this place -- including Redwood -- are black ops. Nothing we do is on the books. Some of it was questionable to begin with. The only universal line we have is that we don't hurt children. If we torture someone, there has to be a good reason. And, yes, a few of us have tortured and killed women."

I just looked at him, waiting for... something. Something more from him to disgust me, something that made me cringe that he'd just admitted to torturing women. He'd said there had to be a good reason.

"You're not a bad person, Ringo. I believe that Redwood is the exception rather than the rule. Otherwise, there'd be more people here trying to either kill me or help Borris get me back. You know your club better than me and know if you have doubts about any of them, but everyone I've had significant interaction with support each other." This was the one conversation he could have started to bring me out of the panic gripping me since Redwood's attack. "I believe in you, Ringo. I believe in Apple and Lemon and Dom. And I believe Rocket is not the type of man to let this go. I'm betting Rocket is currently raising hell because he doesn't seem like the kind of man to let anything go down in his club he doesn't sanction."

"He is scouring every single person in this club right now. He'd already had our tech guys working on it because of things that happened when Lemon got here, but he's pulled everyone in to work only on this. I've never heard him so angry. And that was only from the short interaction I had with him after I killed Redwood.

"I've done bad things, Calista. Killed more people that I care to think about. Some of the things I've done for the government would get me killed and probably rightly so. Though I would never hurt an innocent, especially a child, I can't honestly say that some of what I've done didn't have collateral damage. Maybe not directly, but anytime government upheaval happens, someone innocent gets hurt. So, don't even think I'm a good guy. I'm not."

I studied Ringo for a long time. His gaze never wavered from mine. He didn't say anything else to convince me he and his club were bad people. Which told me they had *really* done some bad shit. Also, he believed this was going to make a difference in how I saw the club. And him.

"What are you trying to say, Ringo? I'm not going to think you're a bad person. After everything you've done for me since I got here, after you taking care of me and showing me how a man should treat a woman, if you think any of your past is going to turn me against you, you're dead wrong." I cupped his face in my hands. "You're a good man, Ringo. Nothing you tell me is going to change that."

He sighed. "Mitch."

"What?"

"My name. Mitch Glout. It's not the name I was born with, but it's the only name I have now."

"Mitch."

"Yeah."

"Mitch." I thought about it for a moment. "Ringo."

"Either one, baby. As long as you call me yours." He pulled me in for a slow, gentle kiss. When he pulled back, he continued, "All the shit I just told you, all that means there will always be people trying to find us. To kill us. If that means they infiltrate our ranks, we will kill *anyone* we have to. Even if it's someone we respected and trusted with those people most precious to us." He brushed my bottom lip with his thumb. "This is why we've always kept to ourselves. Sure, some of us go out in public from time to time, but we've got plans in place to protect us. And now our families."

"See?" I smiled at him. "You're not a bad person. None of you are. If you were, you wouldn't care what happened to anyone but yourself or your brothers. You certainly wouldn't take their side over those of us you haven't known long." I chuckled. "And Lemon, most certainly, wouldn't be vice president."

He snorted out a laugh. "Yeah. She'd have killed us all long before now."

"I thought she'd only been here a few months."

"Yep. Six months." He raised his eyebrows, his eyes wide like he was shell shocked or something. "Seems much, much longer."

I couldn't help it. I laughed, pulling myself close against him and tightening my arms around his neck. "What will you give me not to tell her that?"

He froze, unwinding my arms from around his neck. This time, his expression was almost pleading. "Calista…"

I grinned. "Well?"

"Name your price, wench," he growled. But I could see the mirth dancing in his eyes.

"I'll think about it and tell you later." I leaned in to kiss him once more. He took control and deepened the kiss and I let him. No matter how often he kissed or touched me, I loved it more and more.

"Baby girl." He said it with such affection as he tucked a lock of hair behind my ear. "Let's get you to Bullet so he can examine you. I want to get the blood washed off your hands and arms."

I looked at one of my hands and realized it was covered with blood. Redwood's blood. Immediately, I jerked my hands back. "I'm so sorry," I whispered. The whole evening coming back in a flood. I'd forgotten for a short time what had just happened. "Apple… Oh, God!"

"Hush, baby girl."

"But I forgot about Apple! How could I forget --"

He silenced me with a kiss before opening the door to the truck and getting out with me still in his arms. His casual show of strength was at once daunting and arousing. I clung to him shamelessly. I wanted to see Apple, but I was terrified of what I would find.

"You honestly think Lemon wouldn't be raging to the heavens if Apple were anything but safe? She's hurt, yes. But the fact Lemon hasn't razed the city to the ground yet to find Illivich means Apple is still alive. The fact Bullet hasn't had her taken someplace else -- either by truck or a fuckin' helicopter -- tells me Apple might be hurt, but she's not hurt so badly he can't take care of her here."

All I could do was nod my head. I could feel myself spiraling back into fear and despair, wanting to give into all these feelings buried inside me when I had no idea how to process any of it.

"I... stabbed a man, Ringo."

"And I killed him," he said immediately. "I slit his throat on the Goddamned ground, and I'd do it all over again."

"I've never..."

"And I hope you never have to again. But I'm so Goddamned proud of you, Calista. So Goddamned proud! You defended your friend. *Our family*. My woman will always defend her family. That means this club and everyone in it." He set me on the hood of the truck, wedging his hips between my legs. "Listen to me. Grim Road isn't easy. We're a motorcycle club, but so much fuckin' more. We keep to ourselves, keep attention at a minimum. But we hunt those who need hunting. That means there's always the possibility some dumbass will come after us. We will always destroy them. To do that, we need our women willing and able to defend our children and themselves. We'll always come for you. We just need you to hold on till we get there. That means doing exactly what you did with Redwood."

"Apple jumped in front of me, you know. Shoved me out of the way. He was supposed to kill me. Not hurt Apple."

"Apple gets it. I guarantee you, if the same situation happened again, she'd still throw herself into the battle. Would you do any less for her? Or Gina? Or any of the children?"

"No." My answer was no more than a whisper. "Everyone here has been so good to me. I've never known caring like this from anyone other than my mother. I'd protect everyone here with my life. They deserve no less."

He nodded his head in approval. "Good. Now. Let's go see Apple and make a fuss over her."

Chapter Thirteen
Ringo

Apple was understandably shaken. She'd tried to adopt the personality of her sister, but Apple was gentle where Lemon was hard as granite. I wasn't sure what had happened to send her running and for her to try to change her personality, but this was the woman I'd first met. She was strong, but fragile in so many ways.

"I'm sorry," Apple said. "I didn't mean to cause so much trouble."

"Honey, you're no trouble," Bullet was saying even as he worked on her shoulder.

"You saved Calista," Lemon said, holding Apple's hand. She kissed her sister's fingers, showing a rare moment of tenderness. "For that, you can be as much trouble as you want."

"I agree," I said as Calista and I stepped into the room. "I owe you more than I could ever repay, Apple."

Apple's gaze went immediately to Calista. "You're OK?"

Calista nodded, then burst into tears. She hurried to Apple's side and reached out to her but didn't touch her. Instead, she pulled her hand back and looked up at Bullet.

"Will she be all right?"

"Yeah, honey. She will. Our Apple is one tough cookie."

"I'm really not," Apple said. She tugged her hand away from Lemon and reached out to Calista. Calista took it, holding it firmly with both of hers. "I'm so glad you weren't hurt, Calista." Apple looked a little lost. She was clearly in pain but doing her best to be brave about it. "We've got world domination to plan and stuff."

That got a watery chuckle from Calista. "Yeah. We do."

Calista turned her head toward Lemon. "I'm sorry I brought this shit to your club, Lemon."

Lemon waved her off. "Even if you did, I'm not sorry. If we hadn't gotten rid of Redwood now, he might have done worse later." She gripped Calista's shoulder. "You did exactly what you were supposed to do. I won't hear any more about it."

"Where's Rocket, Lemon?"

"With Crush and Byte. They've gone to get this Borris Illivitch shithead." Lemon's phone buzzed and she pulled it from her back pocket, checking the message she'd gotten. She gave a derisive snort before putting it back. "'Bout fuckin' time."

"They found him?" Apple looked up at her sister, a hopeful look on her face.

"No. But reinforcements are coming. God have mercy on Illivitch's soul. Because your man will have none."

Apple looked confused. "My... what?"

Lemon shrugged. "Deacon is on the way. And if he doesn't make things right with you, after he finds and kills Illivitch, I'll kill him. Might anyway. So either way, it's a one-way trip for him and he knows it."

"Lemon! What did you do?"

"Nothing you need to be concerned about. Just get better. That's your one job." She reached down and squeezed Apple's shoulder. "Now. Bullet, does she need to go to the hospital?"

Bullet shook his head. "I want to take her to my clinic in town for an X-ray, but I think she's fine." He reached over to a small, curved basin sitting on the table beside the bed where he worked on Apple. He pulled out the bullet he'd obviously removed from Apple's chest before he stitched her up. "Souvenir."

Lemon took it from Bullet before Apple could.

"That's mine, Lemon! Give it back!"

"You'll get it back. I'm having it made into a necklace for you. It'll be a sign that you're a total badass, sis." Lemon grinned wickedly. "You'll thank me later."

"Somehow, I doubt that," Apple muttered. "Anyway, I'm tired of trying to be like you. It's too much work. I want to rest and be pampered and have people wait on me hand and foot." She pouted prettily, but I could see the vulnerability in her eyes.

"Sounds like a plan to me." Rocket entered the room with a kind smile for Apple. "All the women are gathered in your house waiting for you. They'll have everything ready to spoil you by the time you get there. Even got a couple of the brothers volunteering to stay with you until this fuckin' mess is cleaned up."

Apple nodded. "All right," she said in a soft voice.

"I'll even give you some good drugs to help with the pain," Bullet said as he finished dressing her wound.

"How about some of the fruit punch Lemon's always raving about?"

Bullet grinned. "I think I can manage that."

Calista went with Apple to help get her settled and stayed for two days until Apple finally ran her off. The little witch had shot me a text telling me to take my woman home and get her laid. When I'd shown up, Apple had grinned.

"'Bout damned time you came back, Ringo. Take your woman home and fuck her good."

"Apple!" Calista's hands went to her face. Which was now beet red.

"Well? What did you expect? You're smothering me!"

"You said you wanted pampering!" Calista threw her hands up in exasperation.

Apple just shrugged, grinning at Calista. "I did. But you take pampering to a whole other level. I swear, if I have to eat another piece of your cheesecake, I'm gonna puke."

Calista snorted. "So, you hated it, huh?" Yeah. Calista didn't believe that.

"Didn't say that. You keep making it, so I keep eating it."

"I make it *because* you keep eating it. Why didn't you tell me you hated it?" Still, Calista didn't look like someone who'd just been told by her friend that her cheesecake wasn't good, so instead of giving Apple the evil eye, I waited to see what Calista would say next.

"Because I don't. It's the most delicious stuff I've ever had in my life. But in two days you've made three different kinds and I can*not* lay off the stuff."

"Dork."

"Bitch."

They both burst into giggles.

"Call if you need me," Calista said. "Otherwise, I'll see you tomorrow."

"No, you won't," Apple said with a smirk. "At least, you better not." Apple lifted her chin at me. "Bone her one for me, Ringo."

I barked out a laugh. "Where the fuck do you come up with this shit?"

"Have you even met her sister?" Calista raised an eyebrow at me. Yeah. I got it.

"Déjà vu?"

Calista shrugged. "Maybe."

"Stupid question." Apple grinned. "Besides, where do you think Lemon gets it from?"

"You know," I said with a grin. "I can totally believe that."

Once I got her home, Calista plopped down on the bed. "I think I could sleep for a week."

"Wore yourself out?"

"Well, she loved the cheesecake. So I made three different kinds. That last one was so fucking rich I think I gave myself a few cavities."

I pulled off my shirt and dropped it to the floor. "Oh? What kind of cheesecake was it?"

"Um…" She looked guilty as fuck for some reason. "Caramel brownie?"

"Right. The two of you are definitely going to have dentists' bills out the wazoo." I grinned as I continued to strip. "I think I can hear your teeth rotting from over here."

She sat up on the bed, crossing her legs in front of her. "Yeah? Maybe you better gimme something salty to counteract all the sugar."

"Salty, huh?" I couldn't help but laugh. "I got something salty, little witch."

I tugged the waistband of my boxers down and pulled out my cock. Calista's lips parted, watching my cock bobbing in front of her, but she didn't make any move to touch it. Her breath caught as I got undressed.

"I know you said you were tired, but do you think you're up to letting me eat your sweet pussy?"

"Hmm." She grinned at me coquettishly. "I don't know. Sounds a little strenuous."

"Brat." I couldn't help but grin.

"Besides. I had something else in mind."

"Oh?"

"Yeah. There's something I want from you."

"Name it, baby girl." Moving to the edge of the bed, I gripped my cock, stroking lazily.

"I want you to fuck my ass." Even as she said it, she blushed deeply. My woman might be new to sex, but she'd taken to it with gusto. And I, for one, loved it. Pretty sure she did too.

"Wow. That's a tall order from someone who said she could sleep for a week."

"So?" She raised an eyebrow. "Give me a reason to stay awake a while longer."

"Come here." I raised my arms to her. Calista got to her knees and crawled to me. When she reached me, instead of coming into my arms, she lowered her upper body to the bed and enveloped my cock with her mouth.

I grunted, not expecting her to immediately suck me, but not turning her down either. "This first time will be quick. I haven't gotten to fuck your sweet pussy or mouth for two whole days and I need you."

"Mmm..." She hummed happily as she looked up from where she took me into her mouth. What she couldn't fit in, she pumped with her fist. Just like I'd taught her. Once she embraced her needs and was no longer afraid of them, she turned into the most sensual lover I'd ever had. Thank God this woman was mine! She was perfect for me.

I pulled her off me gently. "Lie on your back and let your head hang over the side, baby girl."

She did as I instructed without question. When I fed her my cock, she opened her mouth wide and let me push inside.

"That's it," I praised. "I'm going deep, and you're going to take all of me. Understand?" She hummed around me again. "Touch my thighs if you need me to let up." In response, she slid her hands up to dig her fingers into my ass and pull me forward.

She gagged a couple of times but kept urging me forward. I trusted her to know her own limits and kept moving as she wanted. It wasn't long before she got it down. Then, my balls were hitting her face with every thrust of my cock. All the while, Calista gripped my ass, pulling and pushing, fucking her mouth with my cock at her own pace.

"Gettin' ready to come, baby girl. You don't want it down your throat, push me away now."

She didn't.

When I came, I swore I saw stars. My vision blurred and I bellowed so loud they probably heard me at the main compound. I might have been embarrassed if it wasn't one of the best Goddamned orgasms of my life. But it was. And I wasn't.

I let myself breathe for a couple seconds before pulling out of Calista's mouth and lifting her up, positioning her on her hands and knees at the edge of the bed facing away from me.

Once I had her where I wanted, I latched on to her pussy from behind. She arched her back and cried out and almost immediately dropped her lower body to the bed and spread her legs a little bit farther apart.

I ate her out until she was writhing on the bed and begging me to let her come. Then I took one slow, wet lick from her pussy upward to her ass, circling the little puckered hole with my tongue. The second I did, Calista came unglued, bucking her hips so hard she nearly shook me off.

"What are you doing? Ringo!" She screamed once. Then again, her body erupting in sweat. Every time I showed her something new, she always reacted viscerally.

I gave her little hole one more lick before reaching to the nightstand drawer and pulling out a bottle of lube I'd stashed there for this very occasion. "What do you think I'm doin'?"

"You licked my ass!" The accusing snip to her voice was amusing. Or would have been if I could feel anything other the pressing desire to be inside what I was certain would be the tightest ass imaginable.

All right. I admit. It was still funny.

"Yeah." I chuckled. "I guess I did. Gettin' ready to do somethin' else to that little ass, too."

I spread her cheeks with one hand while I squirted lube between them. Then I wet my fingers and pressed against her ass.

"Ringo!"

"Easy, baby. Push back against me. Let me in."

She did and I slipped first one finger, then two inside her. I did this over and over, lubing my fingers before pushing them back inside her. I soon added a third, stretching her as carefully as I could.

"Now! Please, Ringo! Fuck me!"

I smacked my free hand down on one cheek of her ass and she yelped, glaring back over her shoulder at me. "Who's in charge?" It was a demand more than a question.

"You're fixing to find out who's in charge," she snapped.

So I smacked her ass again. This time, she hissed at me.

"You think you're ready for me for me to fuck this ass?" I bared my teeth at her. "Huh?"

"Do it! Fucking do it *now*!"

Instead, I slid my dick inside her pussy, pounding into her several times as hard as I could. She screamed, her pussy quivering around me, close to coming but unable to push herself over.

When she reached between her legs to stroke her clit, I grabbed her arms, pinning them to the small of her back as I continued to fuck her.

"God! Please, Ringo! I need to come!" Her pleas were the sweetest music.

"No," I bit out. I wanted her so close to the edge she was mindless with lust. She needed to be on the very edge of madness, so I didn't hurt her. Besides, I loved it when she got like this. There was no pretense or attempt to stifle her reactions from me. Probably because I'd made no secret from the beginning that I relished her cries of pleasure.

It wasn't until the first sobs escaped her throat that I stopped. Pulling out of her pussy, I found the lube again and squirted a generous amount onto my cock and coated it with my hand. Then I squirted some inside her, working two fingers inside her to make certain she was ready.

With one hand on her hip and the other around my cock, I guided myself inside her with a slow, steady glide. Backing out, I thrust forward again, deeper this time. It took two more tries before I was fully seated inside her. Sweat coated her body and she thrashed mindlessly.

Then I fucked her.

Calista's cries were loud and sweet. All I could do was give her what she wanted because to deny her would be to deny myself and fuck that shit. I did try to go easy on her, but the woman simply wasn't having it. She reached back with both hands to grip my thighs and pull me to her, her nails digging into my flesh when I didn't move fast enough to suit her.

When I knew I couldn't take any more, I wrapped my arm around her waist to find her clit. I stroked once... twice... And her asshole contracted around my dick and threatened to strangle me. Cum erupted from my dick. Deep inside Calista's ass. Inside her body. Always inside her. Except when I wanted to be especially dirty. It never mattered how I came, Calista enjoyed my orgasm as much as she did her own. Every time I watched her when I came, there was a wonder and delight on her lovely face I'd never seen from anyone before. It was always beautiful. *She* was beautiful.

When we'd both finally settled, I helped her more fully on the bed and settled her on her stomach before I stumbled to the bathroom on wobbly knees to clean up. I brought back a wet cloth to gently clean her pussy and ass before falling into bed with a groan.

"What's the matter, Gramps?" Calista teased, but I could tell she was as tired as I was. "Can't keep up with the youngster?"

"You'll pay for that, little brat. But if you think you can climb on top of me and ride me, knock yourself out. Just don't expect me to do much other than get hard. Little bastard has a mind of his own, and he's tryin' to take what little strength I have left."

She giggled and slid her thigh up mine. With a little sigh, she managed to settle herself on top of me. She guided me inside her pussy and flexed her hips a couple times before settling.

"Whelp," she breathed out. "I tried."

"Yeah, babe. You did." I chuckled softly. "Just stay like this. We can finish later."

"I'm good with that." She was silent, her breathing steady and even. I thought she'd fallen asleep, but then she asked me a question. "What's happening with Borris right now? Did they catch him?"

"Last I heard, Deacon from Iron Tzars MC found him. They have him in a cell somewhere interrogating him. Seems you weren't the only woman he was selling. Or sold. Rocket is working with Sting of the Tzars and they're determined to get every single name the man knew in that business."

"Sounds… unpleasant." She didn't move or even open her eyes. We could have been talking about the weather.

"Yeah. We're hard core here at Grim Road. All of us. But from what Dom's told me, what's happening now is particularly gruesome."

Again, she was silent for so long, I thought she'd finally drifted off. "Does it make me a bad person to hope Borris is getting the same as he dished out? Because, if it does, then you've tied yourself to a really, really bad person."

"No, babe. It don't make you a bad person. At least, no more than it does me. 'Cause hopin' like hell that's what's happenin' right now."

"Thanks. For everything, Ringo. You're a really good man. I'm proud to be yours."

"Proud to be yours too, baby. I'll always be proud to be yours. And to have you as mine."

Finally, she was still, her body relaxed as sleep came. I stroked her back lazily with my fingertips. This woman… This one small woman… She was the key to my heart. The woman I…

"Ringo?" Her voice was a contented, breathy whisper.

"Yeah, baby."

"I love you."

Those words hit me like a punch to the gut. "Baby?"

She tilted her head up to look at me. "I love you,

Ringo."

I searched her eyes for a long time, not daring to hope she meant what she was saying. But I could tell she was.

My lips spread in a slow smile. "I love you too, Calista. I love you too."

Marteeka Karland

International bestselling author Marteeka Karland leads a double life as an action romance writer by evening and a semi-domesticated housewife by day. Known for her down and dirty MC romances, Marteeka takes pleasure in spinning tales of tenacious, protective heroes and spirited heroines. She staunchly advocates that every character deserves a blissful ending.

Marteeka finds joy in baking and gardening with her husband. Make sure to visit her website to stay updated with her most recent projects. Don't forget to register for her newsletter which will pepper you with a potpourri of Teeka's beloved recipes, book suggestions, autograph events, and a plethora of interesting tidbits.

Marteeka at Changeling: changelingpress.com/marteeka-karland-a-39

Want more? Wanda Violet O. is Teeka's Dark Erotica side.

Bones MC Multiverse
Contemporary MC and Crossovers
Bones MC
Shadow Demons
Salvation's Bane MC
Black Reign MC
Iron Tzars MC
Grim Road MC
Bones MC Legends
Kiss of Death MC

Print and Audio
Bones MC Print Duets
Bones MC Audio
Salvation's Bane MC Audio
Iron Tzars MC Audio
Grim Road MC Audio
Kiss of Death MC Audio

Changeling Press LLC

Contemporary Action Adventure, Sci-Fi, Steampunk, Dark Fantasy, Urban Fantasy, Paranormal, and BDSM Romance available in e-book, audio, and print format at ChangelingPress.com -- MC Romance, Werewolves, Vampires, Dragons, Shapeshifters and Horror -- Tales from the edge of your imagination.

Where can I get Changeling Press Books?

Changeling Press e-books are available at ChangelingPress.com, Amazon, Apple Books, Barnes & Noble, Kobo, Smashwords, and other online retailers, including Everand Subscription and Kobo Subscription Services. Print books are available at Amazon, Barnes and Noble, and by ISBN special order through your local bookstores.

ChangelingPress.com

www.ingramcontent.com/pod-product-compliance
Lightning Source LLC
Chambersburg PA
CBHW070446260626
47161CB00004B/1217